Saving the Date

After a vicious gay bashing, Morgan has spent the last three years working hard to survive and thrive. His latest plan? Using Madame Evangeline's high-end dating service, 1NightStand, to take the anniversary of the worst night of his life and replace it with a good—and maybe even sexy—memory.

Zach, a police officer with the Hate & Bias Crime Unit, is still coming to terms with his divorce and struggling to move on with his life. Using a matchmaking service is so very not his style, but sometimes a guy has to trust his friends—even if they don't know everything about him, and he's not sure they ever will.

Face-to-face, however, it becomes clear that despite an attraction, there's a problem. Morgan and Zach have already met—three years ago. But with some courage, a couple of pairs of skates, and a leap of faith? Morgan and Zach have a shot at saving more than one day. Together? They might just make a future.

the reproduction or utilization of this work, in whole or in part, in any form by any electronic, mechanical or other means now known or hereafter invented, is forbidden without the written permission of the publisher.

Published by Decadent Publishing Company, LLC
Look for us online at:
www.decadentpublishing.com

Dear Readers,

We decided to write a novella together a year and a half ago (Angela: Almost two years! May 2016!). As often happens life pops up and things change, but over that time we've grown and learned and changed, much as you do in any relationship.

Morgan is very much a creation of 'Nathan and Zach is very much Angela's character and together they are an amazing team that we adore. We hope you love Zach and Morgan as much as we do!

Want more from these characters? Keep your eyes peeled for Saving the Hounds, Amy & Jasper's story.

'Nathan & Angela

Decadent Publishing Recent Releases

King of Her Heart by TL Reeve
So Not a White Knight by Starla Kaye
Treasure Me by Heather Long
Unexpected Gifts by Sarah and Shannen Brady
Out of Orbit by Thea Landen
Awake: Unsleeping Beauty by Louisa Bacio
If You Can't Stand the Heat by Taryn Kincaid
The Ambassador's Daughter by Venus Cahill
Safe at Home by Wendy Burke
Double Down by Desiree Holt
All I Want by Eden Ashe
Dressing Lily by Siobhan Shannon
One Night in Jersey by Tianna Alexander
Guardian of the Angels by Ashlyn Chase
Sorority Row by TL Reeve and Michele Ryan
The Vessel by Nancy Fraser
Return to Ecstasy by Tina Donahue
Beyond the Veil by Courtney Sheets
Blown Away: Detonate by D.L. Jackson
Blown Away: Explosive Affairs by D.L. Jackson
Downstroke By Desiree Holt
Conquer the Demon by Shiela Stewart
The Danegeld by C.L. Hadyn
Life, Love, and Geekery by Monica Corwin

Also by Angela S. Stone

Duty, Honor, Sacrifice
Duty, Honor, Love
Goalie Interference
Unsportsmanlike Conduct

Dedication

'Nathan:

For everyone walking back out of the minefield.

Angela:

;

Because this isn't the end, it's the beginning.

Saving the Date

By
Angela S. Stone & 'Nathan Burgoine

Chapter One
Morgan

"I think I have a plan," Morgan said.

Morgan's therapist, Theresa, smiled her Cheshire grin. He'd come to love and hate that grin. He loved it because it meant she listened.

He hated it for the same reason.

"For the fifteenth?" she said.

To say Dr. Macedo had his number would be understating things a bit. He'd have gotten nowhere without her, but that didn't make her ability to figure out what he meant from thin air any less disconcerting. She'd helped him through a ton in the last three years—not the least of which had been the first and second anniversary of his bashing—and he'd learned when she pulled out the Cheshire grin, she was open to hearing his plan.

And ready to point out any potential flaws he hadn't considered.

"Yes," Morgan said. "I was thinking about the whole Christmas for Misfit Toys party thing my friends do."

"Christmas for Misfit Toys?" Theresa raised one eyebrow. "Do we need to have the don't-refer-to-yourself-negatively discussion again?"

"It's tongue-in-cheek, I promise. It's the party we take turns throwing for us queerlings who haven't got a family holiday to welcome us. Have I never called it that before? That's what we named it. It's evolved into a pretty big party. And it occurred to me I'm ready for that."

"You'd like to have a party? On the fifteenth?" Theresa's tone had softened, which gave him confidence.

"Yes," Morgan said. "Well, no." He shook his head. "Not a party. But…I want to go out. I want to do something else. I don't know. Basically?" He leaned forward, knowing he wouldn't shock Dr. Macedo. "I'm ready for a date. Preferably a sexy date."

Theresa tapped her chin. They'd discussed all manner of personal details in the last three years. Morgan's body image after acquiring scars noticeable enough to garner comment. The conflicted emotions around sex and attraction, given the kind of man Morgan found attractive, conflated with the image of the man who'd beaten him.

"So, you're organizing a date?" she said.

Morgan shook his head. "No. I guess I figured I'd hit a bar. Dance. I'm not going to drink." He held up a hand, forestalling that particular objection before she could make it. "But I want an organic opportunity to meet someone, and maybe—if it goes well—take them home." He shrugged. "Then, next year, when the day rolls around, maybe I could remember the date instead of the bashing. Or at least as well as. What I want out of this is a stronger memory."

Theresa leaned back in her chair. She tapped her lips with one finger. She smiled.

Morgan felt a tension he'd been trying hard not to show release from deep within his chest. His shoulders relaxed, and he found himself smiling back at her.

"I'm proud of you," she said.

Morgan wasn't sure what he'd been expecting, but those words weren't it. His eyes filled, and he had to swallow, hard. "You are?"

"Morgan, you've worked your butt off. First your physical recovery, and then even harder through your emotional recovery. It's safe to say I've never met anyone as willing as you to face your demons and do what you had to do. I'm pleased to see you taking this step. You've got a healthy awareness of your own limitations, and I happen to agree. This could be a decent way to rob the anniversary of some power."

Morgan grinned.

"However...."

His grin evaporated.

She held out her hand. "No, hear me out. I'm not disagreeing."

"Sorry," he said.

Her smile returned. She leaned back and opened the top drawer of her desk. "I'm not sure a random potential hook-up is the way to go."

"Okay." Was it weird to hear the sixty-year-old woman say "hook-up"? Yes. But more to the point, if a bar night wouldn't cut it, then what? He didn't want to use an app. Too many built-in assumptions about where the night would lead. He wanted the opportunity to bail.

Just in case.

"As you know," Theresa said, "I do a lot of work with sexual assault survivors, and I'm also involved with sexual advocacy work for persons with disabilities."

Morgan nodded. It had been one of the reasons he'd been referred to her. He'd never had a surfeit of positive body image, always felt too skinny, and the less said about being a freckled ginger, the better. Toss in scars, physical therapy, and the reality of having the crap beaten out of him and being left to bleed in the snow by a guy who'd inspired the thought, "*Wow, he's hot*," prior to the attack?

Well. Sex had become a minefield.

But Dr. Macedo had walked him out of it, with only one or two explosions along the way.

From the drawer, she pulled out a small, elegant business card, tapping it once on the top of the desk before offering it to him. Morgan took the card and read it.

"Madame Evangeline?" He raised his eyebrows. "Madame? As in...?"

"It's a matchmaking service," Theresa said. "But if you're asking for a memorable night, trust me when I say you'd be far better served this way. It's better than leaving things to chance, no?"

Morgan looked at the card. "There's no phone number."

"It's a referral service. Word of mouth." She smiled again.

"So you've...?" Morgan wasn't sure where to go with his question.

"Madame Eve is how I met my husband," she said.

"Wow. Okay. Not trying to get married, though,"

he said. "Like you said, I know where I'm at right now. I'm figuring out how to be good in my own skin."

"I think you're not giving yourself enough credit. Again." She nodded. "But yes, it's a date. And with Madame Eve at the helm? Definite potential for a sexy date."

He nodded, glancing down at the card.

"Okay." He felt a thrill in his stomach. "Yes."

Theresa smiled. "I'll connect you. There's a bit of a questionnaire."

"Is there a checkbox for 'Please no violent bigots'?" he said.

"I promise you, that's not something you'll need to worry about."

Morgan held the card, heart thudding.

Thing was? He believed her.

Zach

"You should burn that photo." Glancing up from the report on his computer, Zach shook his head at his best friend and work partner.

"You've said that every day since the divorce." Locking his computer, he swiveled around to stare at the older man standing next to him. "My answer is still the same."

"Zach, come on. You divorced her over a year ago." Rylie folded his arms over his chest, glaring at him.

"Nine months," he corrected. "Technically."

"You've been split up for the better part of two years, so why is a photo of your wedding day with the BOTN still on your desk?" Reaching out, his partner grabbed the heavy frame and held it away from him.

"Give it back, Lancaster," he snapped, holding his hand out. "And don't call her BOTN." Bitch of the North, the nickname the squad had given his ex, once the whole cheating-on-him-with-his-boss affair came out. She'd divorced him then his boss had transferred to another unit and married her. They'd just had a baby.

"On one condition." He flashed him that shit-eating, I'm-about-to-cause-trouble-like-you-wouldn't-believe grin.

He waited, hoping to win out a brief staring contest before sighing. "What is it?"

"Go on a date on Sunday afternoon." Not a question, a statement.

"No."

Rylie started to walk away. "Okay, then."

"Ry!"

Turning around, his partner grinned at him even wider. "Yes?" he asked, with far too sweet a tone.

"I'll think about it."

Returning to his desk, Rylie set the photo down. "Her name is Morgan. She loves books, rock climbing, kayaking, hockey, and skating. You're meeting her on Sunday at two at Lansdowne. Bring your skates."

"The canal might not even be open," he argued. The weather had been mild for winter, hovering above zero for most of December and the first week of January. Although, they currently endured a cold snap.

"NCC opened the stretch between Bank Street and Somerset today. Should be even more open by Sunday...." his friend teased. He knew how much he liked skating on the canal, and rock climbing. Heck, any outdoor activity, especially since his ex-wife had been a sit-on-the-couch-and-watch-TV-every-night kind of person. He hadn't even made it out last year between the shortest skating season ever, and promotions, and his ex.

Zach chewed his lower lip. It had been ages since he'd had a date, if you didn't count—and he didn't—the disastrous evening with the woman who turned out to be twenty-five years older than her profile photos had suggested. He had no interest in going out with a lady in her sixties.

"How do you know this girl?" he asked.

For the first time, he hesitated. "I don't."

"So, you're trying to set me up on a blind date, and you don't even know the chick? Not happening." He turned back to his computer.

"Amy knows her," Rylie blurted.

He paused mid-password. Amy, Rylie's younger sister. Heck, he thought of her as a kid sister, too, with all they had been through together in the last two years: his ex, her leaving her abusive boyfriend and moving back to Ottawa. He owed her his life, and he would do anything for her, even go on a blind date. Sighing, he spun back around and waited for his friend to continue.

"You know Amy used that dating service last year to meet that guy, right?"

He nodded. "Jasper?"

"Yeah, well she used this dating service run by a lady called Madame Eve—"

"Like a madam, as in sex trafficking and prostitution madam?"

"No!" He snapped, "Do you think I'd let Amy get involved in something like that? It's a professional title or something. She runs a super-elite dating service, and Amy thinks you've been moping around far too long. She wants you to be happy. I want you to be happy. Heck, the entire unit is tired of you moping."

"If I go on this date, you have to promise not to bother me about dating or moving on for an entire year."

"Deal. Amy will call you with the details." Rylie spun on his heel and headed back to his desk. Resisting the eye roll, he returned to his report.

An hour later his office phone rang, and he answered it with a curt, "Hate Crimes, Sergeant Boyd."

"Zachy!" Amy's voice made him smile, even if his best friend had half blackmailed him into going on a date.

"What's up, Amy?"

"Ry told me you're interested in meeting Morgan," she singsonged.

"If only so you'll stop bugging me about dating," he quipped.

"Pfft, who said anything about dating? Madame Eve's service is called 1Night Stand for a reason, honey—you need to get laid."

The words processed for a moment before he sputtered, "Isn't that how you met Jasper?"

"Uh-huh, but do you think I'm going to tell my big brother? Hell no! He still thinks I'll be a virgin on my wedding night! Fat chance of that." She giggled. "Morgan sounds great. You're going to meet her at the new Cakes and Coffee in Lansdowne Sunday, two o'clock. Bring your skates for the canal! Also, I've booked you a room at the Castillo Chateau downtown. Coffee, romantic skate, maybe a Beavertail, and if you end your skate at the hotel...so be it."

"I'm not sure if I should hate you or congratulate you on being an evil genius. Wait. Does Morgan know this is meant to be a.... One off?"

"I would assume so. I knew."

"And you still did it?"

She giggled again. "More than once! Trust me, okay? Eve will find you the perfect person for a roll in the hay."

He groaned. "I don't want to know."

"Ha! Love you, Big Brother 2.0!" She hung up, and he had to stifle another groan as he replaced the receiver.

What the heck had he gotten himself into?

Chapter Two

Zach

Fuck.

Banging his head on the steering wheel, he inched forward. Why had no one told him the 67s had a game today? Add the canal being open, and it made for traffic chaos at Lansdowne.

Zach inched forward again and put his blinker on, finally getting to the gate attendant who asked, "Did you pre-pay?"

"I am here to meet someone at the new Cakes and Coffee," he said, hoping he didn't have to go find impossible parking somewhere on Bank Street.

"Stay to the left and go to the far side of the Wholefoods, there should be a few spots reserved for shoppers," the attendant explained before letting him down the ramp into the garage.

Driving through the lot as fast as he dared, thanks to the red and green indicator system, he located a spot near the movie theatre. Grabbing his bag, which included a few supplies he had thrown in in case this date went well, plus his skates, out of the trunk, he took the elevator topside.

The minus twenty-five degree wind chill knocked the breath out of him as he went out into the cold. Wrapping his scarf tighter and bending his head downward against the wind, he made his way over to the new Cakes and Coffee in the far quarter of Lansdowne Park.

He had been to their Byward Market location a few times, but he'd avoided the new Lansdowne development like the plague. Lack of parking plus not in my back yarders, or NIMBYs, made the place a bit of a nightmare. Hurrying past people queuing for Beavertails, he made his way to the coffee shop. When he opened the door, a blast of heat rushed out. He opened the inner door and entered the sleek, modern coffee shop.

Unwrapping his scarf, he focused in on the couch in the far corner where his date should have been sitting. Instead, an attractive redhead had his head buried in a book.

Checking the text message from Amy, he re-read it for the billionth time.

Green couch, 2 p.m. Red hair, reading a copy of Dancer from the Dance.

The guy on the couch fit that description. Unsure,

he made his way to the counter and ordered a coffee in a to-go cup.

As he stirred in the required amount of cream and sugar, his phone rang. He checked the caller ID. Amy.

"Yeah?" he answered.

"Why aren't you there yet?" she growled at him.

"I—"

"Morgan is getting ready to leave." He glanced at the redhead on the couch. The guy appeared a little dejected, staring at his phone.

Attraction pulled at his solar plexus.

"Almost there," he lied. "Got stuck in traffic."

"Hurry up," she snapped. "Eve is pissed."

"Tell her I'm sorry." He wanted to ask about Morgan. His brain screamed not to ask, but he did anyway. "Amy, Morgan is a girl right?"

"Of course! Why would Eve set you up with a guy?"

"Never mind. Gotta go. Will talk later." He hung up on her because he couldn't talk more due to the pounding in his chest.

The phone belonging to the young man on the couch dinged, and Zach stared at him, watching as relief washed over his face. He looked fucking adorable, not too built, with a smattering of freckles. The thought of what he could do to him went straight to his dick.

He could walk out right now, and no one would know, or he could go ask the guy his name.

His heartbeat pounded in his ears. No one knew he played both sides of the field, not Rylie, certainly not Amy, heck, not even his ex-wife knew. He hadn't been with another guy since college, and his dick reminded him, pressing against the zipper of his jeans.

Then again, he could be wrong. He took a quick stock of the room. No other redheads, not even anyone with dyed red hair.

Taking a sip of his too-hot coffee, he burned his tongue but didn't care. The door jangled, and in walked a pretty attractive guy, tall, slim-ish, with dark-blond hair. The redhead lit up like a Christmas tree, only for his face to fall when, about thirty seconds behind the blond, a cute brunette entered the shop and, immediately, the man leaned down and kissed her.

Going back to his phone, he stared at it then glanced again at the door.

Dammit. Even if he wasn't sure about a date with a guy, he couldn't let him think no one showed. He had the expression of a just-kicked puppy.

Taking a deep breath, he walked over to the chair

next to the couch, set his bag down, and pulled off his hat and gloves then stuffed them into his pocket.

"This seat taken?" he asked.

The redhead glanced at him, eyes widening.

"N-no," he stammered.

The redhead stared at his phone, giving him a few sidelong glances. A copy of the correct book sat on the table next to his half-drunk coffee.

Fuck it.

"Sorry, you're not Morgan, are you?" he asked, his voice lacking his usual confidence.

The redhead's big hazel eyes rounded. "Are you Zach?" he whispered.

Morgan

So far, so not good.

Morgan put his book down and picked up his phone. He'd done the surveys—and good Lord what thorough surveys—and he'd had an email exchange with the rather formal Madame Evangeline on a few details. The meeting spot had been picked, along with the room at the chateau, which somehow didn't seem presumptive, though Morgan hoped it might be.

The café hummed. He'd gotten here way too early, taking the bus before the one he'd needed, and had camped out where he'd said he would be, book in hand, toque stowed in his backpack, and nothing but nerves and tea between him and the upcoming date with Zach.

Who was now officially late.

Every time the door opened, Morgan held his breath. He'd never noticed how hidden someone's features were when the person bundled for an Ottawa winter. He felt a little stupid waiting to see if any of the men would look back at him, or if they'd reveal blond hair under their various winter hats.

He'd been pretty sure Zach had arrived about five minutes ago. The guy—scratch that, the very big guy—had come in and scanned the room, definitely making eye contact with him. And *zing*! Or had Morgan imagined the zing? But then the guy had taken off his hat—blond, check—and gone to get a coffee instead of coming over. Now, not-Zach sat on the other side of the café, not glancing up, or checking his phone, or giving any sign of waiting for someone else.

Maybe it *was* Zach. Maybe one look had been enough to decide "no way," and Zach would just wait for Morgan to give up and go—

You're insane.

He grabbed his phone and tapped.

I know it's only five minutes past the meeting time, Morgan wrote. *But have you heard if maybe our evening had to be canceled at the last minute?*

It would suck, but it would be better than being stood up.

Not to my knowledge, came Madame Eve's nearly instant reply. *I do apologize. Let me look into this.*

Morgan exhaled. *Crap.* Okay, maybe this had been a terrible, terrible idea. He wondered if tall, blond, and oblivious over there was Zach. It didn't seem so unlikely now. Would it kill the big guy to come over and say, "Sorry, not interested"?

No further response to his text came. He put the phone down and picked up his book.

I'll be the ginger in the corner, reading. And in case there are two redheads reading books, I'll be reading Dancer from the Dance.

That's what he'd sent to Zach. He wished they'd set it up for him to initiate the contact instead. He tried to read again. He'd see what Madame Evangeline had to say and finish his tea. If Zach hadn't come by then....

He'd burn that bridge when he got to it.

"This seat taken?"

Morgan looked up. The very big guy stood over him. Also very handsome, from the tiny bit he could see, anyway. Nice eyes. Great mouth.

Wait. He'd asked a question, hadn't he?

"N-no." It came out in staccato. He tried not to flinch. When the big guy didn't say anything else or move to sit down, Morgan went back to his book, and tried not to check him out more than once every, oh, thirty seconds. If this *was* Zach, he owed Theresa something good. Like, a bouquet of flowers. Or chocolate. Were there such things as chocolate flower bouquets? Of course, there'd be no need for a thank-you gift if the guy never looked at him or spoke to him again. He hadn't even sat.

"Sorry, you're not Morgan, are you?"

He speaks. Morgan blinked. "Are you Zach?"

The big guy nodded. "Yeah." He swallowed, as if the word caught in his throat. "I'm Zach."

Okay, the important thing here is not to drool on the table.

"Sorry," he said, fumbling for words of his own. He had to crane his neck to talk to the guy. Had there been a checkbox for "big, Teutonic warrior heritage"? Because it seemed he'd checked it off. "I, uh. Wow. You are tall."

The big guy—his date, Morgan corrected himself— cracked a wan smile.

"Sit down." Morgan gestured to the empty chair. "Please."

Zach hesitated for another second—Morgan tried to convince himself the blond wasn't looking for a reasonable escape plan—then pulled out the chair and sat down. No amount of padding could account for the width of the man's shoulders.

Morgan exhaled. "So. On a scale of one to a billion, how awkward is this?"

Zach seemed to surprise himself with a laugh. "You have no idea. I'm sorry I'm late. Traffic. And, uh.... There's something...." He frowned. The intensity of his gaze unnerved him.

"Do I have something on my face?" He'd not ordered hot chocolate to avoid whipped cream accidents.

Zach blinked. "Sorry. No. I'm...." He shook his head. "Would you believe you look familiar?"

"Like your dead girlfriend?" Morgan grinned, singing the words.

"Excuse me?" Zach leaned back, frowning.

"Oh. Not a *Rent* fan, eh?" Morgan held up his hands. "Sorry. When I'm nervous, I become a font of inappropriate humor. I'm told it's endearing. Y'know, by, like, my misfit friends." Morgan bit his lip. "Which probably means it's not endearing, come to think of it."

Zach stared at him.

"It's a line from a musical," Morgan said. "And I'll stop now." He clenched his jaw shut before he could say anything else.

Zach took a deep breath. "Were you expecting…? Uh. I mean, did…?" He didn't meet Morgan's gaze, and he rubbed his thumb up and down his coffee cup. He had a little scar through his eyebrow, and—

"Wait," Morgan said. When Zach raised his eyebrows, the familiarity faded, but it had been there. "Maybe I do know you. Do you ever shop at Urbane Myth? It's a consignment shop in the Village. You'd never forget Phoebe, the owner. She's a glamazon. I'm less memorable."

Zach shook his head. "No. I don't know it."

Morgan frowned. "Okay. What about you? Where do you work?"

Zach cleared his throat, shifting in his seat. No way could the big guy be comfortable in the little chair. "I'm a cop."

Oh no. Oh for the love of…. "A cop."

Zach nodded, then added, "With the Hate and—"

"Bias Crimes Unit."

They stared at each other.

"On a scale of one to a billion?" Zach said. "We just hit a billion."

Chapter Three

Zach

Color drained from the younger man's face. Running though his recent cases, Zach hadn't seen him in the last year. Not since his promotion, so, from an ethics standpoint, he didn't have to leave right now.

But *fuck*. What were the chances? A victim he'd met in his three years with the unit.

"I...." He hesitated, not wanting to get himself into a situation he couldn't back out of. Morgan already appeared shaky. "Umm. When—"

"Three years ago." The pain of whatever happened to him clouded his face. "Three years ago, today."

"I'm sorry," he said, more automatically than out of sympathy. He racked his brain, hard. It would have been his first month. After only a month and a bit as a detective, he wouldn't have been lead on any of the cases, but observing and note taking.

Morgan stared at him, a deer in headlights. Scared, no, near terrified of him. Or maybe his own past.

"I have to be honest. I don't remember your case or any details about it. I was a rookie trying to figure out my new job. We don't have to talk about it if you don't want to. If it makes you feel uncomfortable, I can leave right now." He paused. "Or, if you want, we can go skating and get to know each other. The conditions are supposed to be near perfect." He waited, his stomach twisted into knots. He'd taken a huge, stupid, risk by talking to the adorable redhead, and now it was all for naught.

The younger man chewed on his bottom lip before responding. "Yes."

"I understand." Trying not to feel dejected, he pushed to his feet and zipped his jacket. Scooping up his bag, he moved to turn away.

"Zach, wait."

He paused again.

"I meant, yes. I want to go skating with you."

The nerves in his stomach settled. "Okay, then. We should get going." He glanced at his watch. "We only have about an hour and a half till it's dark."

"Sounds great." Morgan stood and gathered his things. They both bundled against the cold then headed outside and toward the canal.

Under the layers upon layers of outerwear, they couldn't have talked to each other if they'd wanted to, not until they shuffled into the warmth of one of the new changing chalets on the ice. Most people seemed to be taking off their gear and heading home. The hut bustled with people, children. He almost stepped on one as he made his way to an open spot in the corner and dropped to a bench. Morgan sat across from him in the busy hut.

"I haven't been on the canal in years." Morgan unraveled his scarf before opening the backpack he carried. He pulled out some battered skates and set them on the rubber-covered floor.

"I play pickup hockey twice a week or so." Zach retrieved his own beat-up pair. "I try and hit the canal at lunch, but last year's skating season was so crappy I didn't make it once, and I haven't been able to make it this year yet either."

Unlacing his heavy boots, he pulled his feet out and took off the thick athletic socks he'd worn out of the house. Usually, he went barefoot when he played hockey, but, with it being minus fifteen plus wind chill, he grabbed a pair of super-thin insulating socks from his bag and pulled them on.

It took him another thirty seconds to lace himself into the skate boot. Morgan, for his part, struggled to pull on the first one.

"Need a hand?" he asked.

Sighing, he nodded. "If you don't mind."

"No problem." Kneeling down in front of his new friend, he put his blade between his knees and pulled his jeans up. As he touched his bare leg, electricity crackled between them. He stared directly at Morgan's obvious and growing attraction toward him.

The redhead blushed, and he dropped his foot, allowing him to adjust himself. In an ice hut full of families, they could not do what he wanted, not in that exact moment, anyway.

Clearing his throat, he asked, "How many socks are you wearing?"

"Three pairs," he replied. "I didn't want to be cold."

"You're never going to get a proper fit on your boot if you have that many layers on," Zach explained. "Here." Pulling the skate off, he peeled away two pairs of socks before replacing the boot and tightening it for him. He did the same with the other one.

"Thank you," the redhead whispered.

"You're welcome. Come on." He stuffed his winter boots into his bag before pulling it over his shoulders, and Morgan did the same. He tilted slightly, and Zach reached out and clasped his hand, steadying him "You okay?"

He nodded. "Just out of practice."

"Hang on to me if you feel unsteady," he replied. "I don't mind."

Morgan blushed but nodded. The pair bundled up and donned sunglasses, more to protect their eyes against the bitter-cold wind than the sinking sun as they headed out into evening. His partner seemed a little wobbly at first, so Zach swung around backward and held out both his hands to steady his date.

"Thanks," he said, muffled under the layers.

"Not a problem," he said, skating backward. "Let me know if I'm going to run into someone," he teased, glancing back to make sure he had a clear path.

The sun starting to go down and the minus twenty-five plus wind chill meant others on the ice were far and few between.

"You're good," Morgan told him from underneath his coverings. "I love skating, but I just don't get enough of a chance to do this."

"I know the feeling," he replied.

Sparks flew between them. He hadn't been expecting this. He'd wanted a cute girl and a quick roll in the hay. Now, he got a cute guy and this. It seemed heavier than a roll in the hay, though, somehow. Not for him, but for Morgan.

They made their way along the canal from Lansdowne toward downtown. About three and a half kilometers and less than forty minutes on a good day. The wind blew hard, at times, making their progress much slower than he would have liked.

Thirty minutes in, his blade caught on a rut, his ankle twisted, and he went down onto his right hip, hard, pulling his partner down with him.

"Fuck," he moaned, not wanting to move for fear he'd done serious damage.

Morgan groaned in pain. "You okay?"

"Yeah." They untangled their limbs, and his hip and right leg protested as he got onto all fours and stretched his leg out, testing before he stood. Once upright, he reached down and helped the younger man to stand. "You all right?"

"You cushioned my fall," he teased.

Two volunteer first aiders headed toward them. Just what he needed. He prayed he didn't know them.

Thankfully, he couldn't recognize them under their own winter gear. "You gentlemen all right?"

"The only thing hurt is my pride." And his hip, but it wasn't worth mentioning to the volunteers.

"Want us to check you out?" a first aider asked.

"I think that's my job," Morgan quipped.

The shorter of the two first aiders laughed, and only then he realized she was female. "All right. Have a good night. Flag one of us down if you need anything," she told them before they skated away.

They were almost to Pretoria bridge. "Did you want to keep going? We're about a kilometer from the next rest area."

"Yeah. I'm having fun," his date replied, pulling the scarf away from his face. "I'm glad the wind direction has changed and it's at our backs."

"That makes a difference," he conceded. "Come on. It's starting to get dark out." Morgan re-bundled himself then grabbed his hand, and they headed toward downtown.

Their strides on the ice were long and confident, despite their fall, and it took less than twenty minutes to make it to the rest area.

Slowing, they headed toward the refreshments.

"Can I buy you a Beavertail?" Morgan asked, gesturing to the iconic red-and-green hut on the canal.

He shook his head. "I hate them."

"Really?"

"Yeah, sorry."

"No, I hate them, too! They're gooey dough and sickly sweet," Morgan said. "I know most people love them, but they're just not for me."

"My best friend loves them, but I can't handle the sugar," Zach agreed. "Want to keep going?"

"Sure."

His partner grabbed his hand this time, and they skated the last kilometer to the Rideau rest area. The sun had almost set, streaky colors of pink and yellow filling the sky as they headed to the change hut to find the room unoccupied.

They picked a spot in the corner of the chalet again. This time, Morgan sat on his right instead of across from him. He unbundled, losing the sunglasses and his scarf. His breath came in shorts pants. They had gotten a good workout on the ice.

"Did you have fun?" He pulled off his skates.

"I did. Is your side okay?" His date undid his laces.

"My hip is sore, but I'll survive. Not the first time I've gone down on the ice. You didn't get hurt, did you?"

He shook his head. "No, just umm...." He cleared his throat and blushed a deep red. Glancing over his shoulder, he did a brief survey of the empty hut before he leaned in and pressed a quick kiss to his lips.

Surprised, Zach didn't respond to the kiss.

Morgan pulled away as if he'd been burned. "Sorry.

You didn't want, I mean...I...."

Leaning in, he kissed the redhead, the only way he could think of to make him stop stammering and convey his intentions. Morgan groaned and reached out, laying his gloved hand on his chest. He went to deepen the kiss, but the creak of the hut door opening broke them apart.

A woman and a pretty girl he assumed to be her teenage daughter came in and picked a spot far from them to undress.

He grabbed his boots out of his bag and went to work lacing them up, trying not to let the younger man see what the kiss had done to his body.

"So, do you, um, have any plans now?" Morgan whispered.

"Well, I heard Eve booked a room at the chateau?" he replied, strategically. "I thought I would go visit...her."

Grinning at him, Morgan nodded. "That sounds like a great plan."

Wiping the ice and wet off of his blades, he shoved them into his bag and waited while his date finished undoing the laces and taking off the skates.

They both rebundled before going out into the cold. Either the light sweat he'd worked up or the sun going down made the wind seem colder as they hurried topside.

Crossing the street to the war memorial, they walked along the perimeter then crossed the street, and then crossed the bridge over the canal locks.

They didn't speak until they entered the marble interior of the chateau. Opened in 1912, the building had been built in the classic gothic style. He'd been inside once before, for a co-worker's wedding a couple of years ago, but the beauty and opulence stayed classic.

The security guard shot them a sidelong stare. The "Do you belong here or are you a dumb tourist?" gaze.

Nodding to him they took off their hats, scarves, and gloves before making their way over to the desk. "What name's the reservation under?" he asked his date.

"Umm, I don't know. I was just told there was a room for us here, if we, uh, wanted it," Morgan replied.

"Good thing we want it," he teased, which made his new potential lover blush dark.

A moment later, a girl appeared out of nowhere, waving them over. "Hello. Bonjour," the girl said.

"Hi, we have a reservation," he replied.

She smiled at them, her fingers poised over the

keyboard. "What's the last name?"

"Uhh, it could be under...."

"Fréchette," Morgan supplied.

She typed it in. "Uh, no sorry."

"Try Boyd," Zach offered.

"I have two under Boyd. What's the first name?"

"Zach."

The front desk girl hesitated. *Fuck.* "Could it be under something else?"

"My full name?" he tried, hoping she wouldn't make him say it out loud.

"Which is...?" She smiled at him in a sickly sweet, obviously fake way.

Fuck. "Ezekiel," he mumbled.

"Of course, Mr. Boyd." She typed a few more keys. "Your room has already been paid for...." She frowned. "I'm so sorry, but they've put you in a king suite. I can try and—"

"King is fine," he growled, annoyed with her over helpfulness.

"I'm pretty sure we have a suite with two queens—"

"I said king is fine," he barked in his cop voice.

"But...."

A tall gentleman in a sharp suit and a badge that

read "manager" quickly crossed from the other side of the large check-in desk. "Thanks for your help, Anna. I'll take it from here," he told her, dismissing her without looking at her.

"Sorry about that, Mr."—he glanced at the screen—"Mr. Boyd. I have you booked into a king suite. The suite has been paid for already by…ah, yes, Madame Evangeline. I will need a credit card for incidentals."

Morgan reached for his wallet. "My treat."

"Sure." Zach shared one of those smoldering, we-are-going-to-fuck-our-brains-out expressions with his date.

"Wonderful. You're in suite 1503." The manager handed them two key cards. "Here you go. Call the front desk if you need anything. To make up for the confusion, I'll arrange for an upgraded romance package from room service. Ring them when you would like it delivered. Tap the cards against the reader in the elevator then select the floor; otherwise, you'll return to the lobby."

"Thank you."

They made a beeline for the elevator.

As soon as the door shut, Morgan started to laugh. "Oh, let me get you two queen beds," he mocked in falsetto.

He chuckled. "She was pretty clueless." He grabbed his date by the jacket and pulled him in, kissing him deeply for the first time. Moaning, he leaned into the kiss for a brief moment before the elevator announced they had arrived at the fifteenth floor, and they sprang apart.

Rushing down the hall. Zach slid his card in the slot, and it blinked red. Trying again, the door blinked green and clicked open.

The second the door to the suite closed, he pressed Morgan against it. Throwing his bag on the floor, he pulled at his date's puffy winter jacket, unzipping it, then slid his hands inside, running over the redhead's slim waist. Pushing the offending clothing item to the floor, he pulled him in close, and they kissed until they were both breathless.

When they pulled apart, struggling to breathe, Morgan made a face at him. "So. Ezekiel?"

"Fuck," he replied. "You heard that?"

"Uh-huh." He tugged at Zach's winter jacket. "Think we can get rid of this?"

"Yup." Shucking his jacket, he tossed it on the floor next to his bag. Pulling the younger man farther into the suite, he kissed him one more time before shoving him onto the sofa in the living room. Stripping off his sweater and shirt, he straddled Morgan's legs then pushed him backward.

But Morgan didn't react the same as before. Instead, he stiffened, breath coming in short, panicked pants, eyes squeezed shut.

"Morgan." He kneeled next to him. "Morgan, squeeze my hand."

He did.

"Take a couple of slow, deep breaths and talk to me."

Morgan slowed his breathing, but his eyes stayed closed.

"Morgan, I need you to look at me."

He blinked impossibly long lashes at him. "I...."

"Panic attack?" he asked, guilt welling up in his chest. *Dammit*. Morgan had told him someone had physically hurt him, and he hadn't thought about it when he tossed him around like a rag doll. He enjoyed being bigger, stronger than a lover, but he hadn't stopped to think how it would make him feel.

"Yes," he replied, still sounding distant.

"Want to talk about it?"

He shook his head.

"I'll get you some water." Feeling as if someone

had punched him in the gut, Zach stood and went into the bathroom, catching a glimpse of himself in the mirror. The black semicolon tattoo on his left inner arm stood out against the rest of his too-white skin; the mark a reminder he had gotten himself in those dark days after BOTN left him when he didn't know if he would make it.

Turning on the taps, he let the cold water run for a moment before filling one of the glasses and carrying it out into the living room area. Morgan appeared pale but more composed.

"Here." He handed him the water.

"Thank you," he whispered.

Sitting next to him on the couch, he hesitated before wrapping his arm around Morgan. "I'm sorry."

"No, I'm sorry," he replied. "I feel stupid."

"Don't. It's my fault. I should have been more sensitive." Zach mentally beat himself up for his actions.

"No, it's mine." Closing his eyes, he swallowed hard. "I got bashed by this really big guy. Like bigger than me, taller than me, stronger than me, and I couldn't do anything. When you started pushing me around, I flashed back to that helpless feeling."

"I'm sorry I made you feel unsafe." Reaching out,

he took Morgan's hand and squeezed it. "What can I do to make you feel safe with me?"

"Not much. Sometimes, it's the way someone moves." He offered a wobbly smile.

Zach kissed him and promised himself he would never hurt him again.

Chapter Four

Morgan

They rose together, continuing the kiss. It felt good. And then Morgan shivered again. They broke apart.

"Okay," Zach said, pulling back. "Okay."

"I'm sorry." Morgan rubbed his arms. He tried to remember all the coping strategies he'd talked over with Theresa, but.... Nothing. Had he screwed this up?

Zach jerked the chair from behind the desk, turned it to face Morgan, and sat.

Morgan blinked. "What are you doing?"

Zach rested both arms on the chair and centered his feet on the floor.

"I won't move."

"What?" Morgan whispered.

"I. Won't. Move." Every word, a promise.

"Zach...."

"Look at me."

Somehow, without his shirt or jacket, Zach appeared larger. He had a pumped chest, wide shoulders, and thick biceps, and darker chest hair than

Morgan would have imagined on the blond man. He radiated strength—exactly the kind of guy Morgan liked. Not chiseled, a big guy who must put some quality time in at the gym, without killing himself for a six-pack. A lug. He even smelled like a lug. Plain soap with a hint of musk.

Details sank in. Zach gripped the arms of the chair, like holding himself in place took no small effort, tension playing in the twitch of the man's thick biceps.

Zach had one little scar on his eyebrow, but, otherwise, the man's body was all but untouched.

He wanted to touch. His fingers twitched at the thought.

"It kills me you're afraid of me," Zach said.

"It's not...." He paused. "I'm not afraid of you. I know, in here"—he tapped his forehead—"you'd never hurt me."

"But."

His face burned. "I know this whole meltdown thing isn't sexy."

"You're sexy." The evenness of Zach's words unnerved him. And held promise.

And Morgan almost believed it. "Thank you."

"I won't move," Zach repeated. He shifted, leaning back. The muscles in his arms flexed. "Come here."

Morgan swallowed. God knew he wanted to. He wanted to feel the hardness of Zach's chest, and find out how soft or rough the hair would be. He took a step closer.

And as promised, Zach remained in place.

He felt stupid, weak, and broken. He turned away, hesitating.

"Hey," Zach said. "Come back to me."

He focused on the floor between them.

"I will never hurt you."

"Okay," Morgan said. "Okay."

He saw no pity in Zach's gaze. No accusation. Heat filled his gray eyes. Hunger. Desire.

Maybe....

He took a single step. Then one more. Zach, true to his word, hadn't moved at all, though he could see the tension lining every muscle in the man's arms and chest.

His fingertips grazed Zach's skin along his left forearm. The hair felt softer than he'd expected, and Morgan's heart started to pound. Not with fear, exactly. He swallowed. He traced a line up Zach's arm and stopped when he saw a small tattoo, almost hidden from sight, high on Zach's forearm.

A semicolon. A simple black semicolon.

Oh. Oh wow. Something gave. Some piece of the hardened, barricaded casing Morgan had built around himself...cracked.

Let him in. The voice could have been Theresa's, or Phoebe's, or even his own.

He couldn't take another full step forward. If he got any closer, he'd be standing between Zach's legs.

He closed the final distance. Zach remained still. Morgan lifted his other hand and lowered it to Zach's chest. His skin felt warm to the touch, and the fine hairs rougher than the ones on his forearms.

His hands shook, but....

Maybe....

Zach's gaze locked on him, but he hadn't so much as turned his neck. Morgan stepped over his thighs and slid onto his lap. He felt the tension and heat—and obvious arousal—of Zach beneath him, but still the big man didn't budge. Morgan ran his hands up and over wide shoulders. Warm, and solid, and....

And no threat.

Morgan kissed him. A tentative kiss at first, but Zach responded, opening his mouth and meeting his pressure in return. Zach's chest rumbled with a low groan, and he answered it in kind.

He broke the kiss, both breathing heavier. Zach's

body tensed beneath him—strong, capable of hurting, capable of doing to him any of the things that had already been done to him, had already broken him.

He wouldn't.

He leaned back and pulled off his own sweater and the T-shirt beneath, desperate to feel his skin against Zach's, and, although the moment he felt air on his skin he knew the chorus of self-doubt would start, he took firm mental hold of himself and told those voices to shut right up.

To his surprise, it worked.

He embraced Zach, eliciting another low rumble deep in the man's chest that felt even better with nothing between them. Morgan wrapped his arms behind Zach's head and kissed him, his heart picking up speed and his dick so hard his jeans were now far from comfortable.

Morgan pulled back, barely an inch of space between their eyes.

Both of them panted.

"Zach?" Morgan managed.

"Yes?" Raw need filled the man's voice.

"I'd like you to move now."

"Thank God." He gripped Morgan's waist and rose, lifting him to his feet and then pulling him close.

"Pants off now?" Zach said, tugging on the front of Morgan's belt.

"Yes. Absolutely. Definitely. Yes." They fumbled at each other's belts between frantic little kisses. When Zach's belt came free, Morgan wanted to cheer. He finally got the man's jeans undone.

Zach, on the other hand, still struggled with Morgan's stylish belt with the double pins. Phoebe had picked it out for him, and he cursed her six different ways.

This wasn't the time or place for a slow, teasing reveal. He nudged Zach's struggling hands away, finished unbuckling, and stepped out of his socks and jeans and boxers as fast as he could, flinging his clothing to the floor. Not elegant, but screw it. Three years was a long, long time.

Zach's eyebrows rose. A smile tugged at the corner of his lips, not mocking, not pitying—hungry.

"Hello, handsome," Zach said.

"You? Naked. Now."

Zach saluted, and the cocky gesture made Morgan bite his bottom lip. Zach managed to get his own jeans off with a little more grace, and when he pulled off his boxers and his cock sprang to attention, Morgan bit harder into his lip.

He was uncut, he was hard, and he was big, and that was about the end of coherent thought before Morgan cut the distance between them, offering up one more kiss. He slid down Zach's big body, stopping to give his neck a nibble, his chest a lick, and then, gripping his thighs with both hands, swallowing as much of his cock as he could in one quick go.

"Oh fuck." He bucked against Morgan's mouth.

Morgan loved having a guy at his mercy like this. He shifted one hand to Zach's shaft and teased the skin beneath his foreskin with his tongue. He loved playing with uncut cocks—their owners always so sensitive.

Morgan went to town, taking as much as he could of the man into his mouth, licking and stroking in tandem, pulling enough to tease, but offer no relief.

"Morgan—"

He hummed around Zach's dick, and the big man reached down and took Morgan's head in his hands. He seemed to be holding on for dear life.

Morgan sucked harder, testing himself as much as he dared, and let Zach's dick come free from his mouth. He held it with one hand and licked his way up and down the length of him with little flicks of his tongue.

He paused, staring all the way up to Zach, who had his mouth open and stared right back down at him.

"I like your dick," Morgan said.

"It likes you back," Zach said. "Come here, before I lose it. That's not how I want this to end."

He rose, and Zach gripped his butt, squeezing. They pressed against each other, their dicks hard and rubbing between their bodies. With short steps between long kisses, Zach walked them to the bed, and when it hit the back of Morgan's legs, he sat.

It put that delicious dick too close to his mouth again, and he couldn't resist. He went down on him again, and squirmed his way onto the bed between licks and sucks.

"Okay." Zach's breath came in short, choppy bursts.

"Sorry," Morgan uttered an unconvincing apology. "Too tempting."

"Uh-huh." Zach followed him onto the bed. They shifted, coming together for another kiss—Zach gave little teasing touches that retreated, inviting him inside and then pulled Morgan to sit on his chest.

"Turnabout is fair play." Zach took him into his mouth.

Morgan gripped the headboard of the king-sized bed, his back arched. Zach didn't lack in the cock-sucking department either. Morgan bit his lip, closed his eyes, and enjoyed the wet heat of Zach's mouth, and the tongue pressed all the right places beneath his length.

When he thought he could trust himself, he opened his eyes and leaned back, balancing on one hand behind him on the bed. With the other, he found Zach's cock—so damn hard—and stroked him.

Zach moaned beneath him.

Morgan bucked on top of him, very close to losing it.

"Zach," he groaned.

The man teased his cock with one more long slide of his mouth then came up for air. "How you doing?"

"Oh, y'know, I'm good." He gave Zach's dick a tug, and the big guy grunted.

"Yeah. Me, too."

"One sec." Morgan slid off the big man, his legs a bit weak. He found his satchel by the door and hurried back to where Zach lay, lazily stroking his hard dick, one arm up above his head, a cocky grin firmly in place

"You're freaking hot, mister," Morgan said.

"Right back at you."

Oddly enough? Morgan believed him. Zach's hard-on added a note of authenticity.

Morgan knelt between Zach's legs and licked his

way up his rigid shaft then smiled, winked, and reached for the satchel. He rolled the condom onto Zach and then pulled out the bottle of lube.

"You came prepared."

"And you didn't?"

Zach had the grace to blush. "Fair point." He took the lube from Morgan and squirted some into his hands. He stroked his cock, poured more lube, and then said, "Come here."

Morgan lay on top of him and they kissed again, while Zach's fingers teased into him, getting him ready. Morgan closed his eyes, relaxing against the pressure of his touch.

He groaned.

Zach broke the kiss. "You okay?"

They pressed forehead to forehead. "If you want me to beg, I'm pretty sure I'll beg." Morgan opened his eyes. "Is begging a thing for you?"

Zach smiled. "No begging required." Still, he fingered Morgan once more, the lube warm, and the whole combining to drive Morgan crazy.

Finally, the tip of Zach's cock butted against his hole, and he resisted the urge to throw a hand into the air or something equally uncool. He shifted, easing back and down onto Zach's cock.

Yeah, it had been a while, but oh, it felt so good. And the man's whole damn body was built big, his cock no exception.

"All right?" Zach said.

"Oh yes." Morgan shifted to a crouch, supporting himself on his hands behind him. Every inch burned, but a good burn—and with a final, shaking exhale, he sank the rest of the way onto Zach's dick.

"Fuck, you feel good," Zach said.

He rocked.

Zach threw his head back, gasping. "I am not going to last long," he warned. "Not if you're going to do that."

"Is that a dare?" Morgan said. "I accept."

Zach gripped his waist and lifted him just enough to give himself room to buck up into the younger man, who swore and gripped the sheets.

"You're on." Zach's cocky grin returned.

Morgan gripped his shoulders and rode him, watching the flush in his neck creep higher and feeling the play of the muscle beneath his hands. Zach bucked up into him in rhythm, and, soon, they were both damp with sweat. Morgan bit his lip, groaned, closed his eyes, tried everything he could to hold on, but Zach's cock rubbed him all the right ways with every one of those little bucks, the perfect balance of strong and gentle, and no way would he last much longer.

He opened his eyes and saw Zach gazing back, breathing hard and clenching his jaw.

"Say when," Morgan said.

"Oh, fuck. When! When!"

Morgan squeezed his ass, and Zach came with a loud cry, gripping Morgan's waist and pushing up into him with a series of rapid thrusts. Morgan gripped his dick and jerked himself.

He blew over Zach's chest, arching with the release.

For a few long moments, they clung together, panting.

"Holy shit," Zach said.

"Yeah." Morgan blew out a breath. "That." He climbed off, wincing.

"You okay?"

"I'm great." Morgan meant it. "Let me clean us up."

He went to the en suite and came back with a warm, wet towel. Zach handled the condom. Morgan wiped them both down then retrieved his phone from his satchel.

"What are you doing?"

"Checking in with the Misfits," Morgan said. "I should have done it when we first got back here, but you took your shirt off, and how can a guy keep thinking straight with Viking beef on display?" He winked.

"Viking beef?"

"That's what the Misfits shall know you as."

Zach frowned. "Who are the Misfits?" He looked nervous.

"Don't worry. It's my friends. They'll worry if I don't check in. We're the Misfits. It would be a cool Jem reference, but it's from the Island of Misfit Toys."

"I have no idea what you're talking about."

"You never saw the Rudolph special at Christmas?"

"I'm not a big fan of television, didn't even have one growing up."

"Oh. Well, it doesn't matter. Christmas for Misfit Toys is a tradition with my friends. We call ourselves the Misfits. It's a thing. We look out for each other, and if we're on our own, we check in."

"You think they'll approve?" His sly, cocky smile returned.

"Of falling into bed with a hot guy? Approve doesn't cut it. They'll want details."

"Details." His voice flattened, and a tiny line appeared between his eyebrows. How could someone so big and burly look so anxious around him?

"Don't worry—no photos, no names. It's more of a chosen family. See, we all had nowhere to go for holidays, and we sort of found each other. Or, Nick and Haruto did. They started it. Phoebe invited me a few years ago, and I've gone ever since. There aren't many rules to being a Misfit, but we watch out for each other. They're a queer family, accepting without any conditions. Well, one big rule: No closets. As Phoebe says every time she puts something amazing together, 'Closets are for clothes.'"

Zach's face fell.

It took a moment for Morgan to click.

Well, shit.

Chapter Five
Zach

"No closets."

The words hurt more than Zach cared to admit. Lying together, naked, the sheets tangled among them, the post-sex talk, which they admittedly should have had before sex, but that didn't matter now. "I'm not out."

"Yeah," Morgan acknowledged. "I just realized that. I'm sorry. The Misfits can cope. Besides, I'm okay with this being only for tonight." His lover leaned in and pressed their lips together. Groaning, he pulled Morgan on top of him. Falling back against the pillow, his partner trailed his hand down, squeezing his cock which started to stir.

At the same time, his stomach growled.

"Hungry?" Morgan asked.

"I think we worked up quite the appetite," he replied. "What's your opinion of room service?"

"As long as I don't have to get dressed." Morgan rolled over onto his back and let out a small moan.

"Sore?"

"Not horribly, but it's been a while."

Propping himself on his elbow, he traced his hands down his chest, which was more or less hairless and covered in a smattering of freckles. He kissed the scar roughened skin on his shoulder. "I guess I'll wear a bathrobe to answer the door then dinner naked in bed?"

Morgan made a face at him. "No food in bed."

"Why not?"

He laughed. "I once dated a guy I was convinced was cheating on me with a girl. He kept having these scratches on his back. I figured fingernails, y'know? One night I slept over, and I woke up with the same scratches."

"What was it?"

"He ate pretzels in bed and would get sea salt crumbs all over, and they would scratch his back in the night. After that?" He shuddered. "No food in bed."

"I guess we can eat in the living room," he conceded.

"Naked?"

"Definitely naked," Zach replied.

"Mmm. Get me...a salad?"

He stared at his naked, except for the sheet, lover. "We're at the chateau—which has some of the best food in the city—and you want a salad?"

"Don't want to have a food baby and then be too full to fuck."

"We're going to fuck again?"

"Maybe more than once, if I have my way," Morgan replied with a grin.

"Then I'll order something light," Zach teased. "I'll get the menu." Climbing out of bed, he sauntered into the living room then returned. After kissing Morgan senseless, he opened the book. "What kind of salad do you feel like?"

His new partner punched his arm. "You kiss me like that and ask me what food I want?"

"Hey, a man's gotta eat," he countered.

Morgan rolled his eyes and flopped against the soft pillows. "Read me the menu."

After hearing the choices, he picked the seafood salad, and Zach went with a club with a side salad. The pleasant girl on the other end of the line informed him it would be thirty minutes, and she would also send the romance package the manager had promised.

Hanging up the phone on the bedside table, Morgan pounced on him. He kissed him and pressed his semi erect cock into his side.

Zach moved away. "So, we have thirty minutes."

"Uh-huh." The smaller man pulled him in close.

"I was thinking we could take a quick shower."

"Oh?"

"You know, so we're ready to go for the next round." Reaching down, he squeezed Morgan's penis, lightly but enough to get a moan out of him. "I can't wait to have you inside me."

"I...." Morgan paused and stared at him, his eyebrows knitting together. "Really?"

"Really what?" he responded, confused.

"Why would you want me to...?" He took a breath before continuing. "You want to bottom?"

"Hey." Zach hugged him in close and kissed him. "Listen," he whispered, pressing their foreheads together. "I think you are beautiful and sexy and smart and funny, and why wouldn't I want to be with you?"

"I thought...I mean, you're sort of a walking, talking wet-dream sort of top, mister. You threw me around like a rag doll and—"

Zach kissed him again.

"Do I like that I'm taller and physically bigger than you? Yes, but it doesn't mean I don't want you to take control sometimes. I like being on the bottom. Actually, I prefer it. I like when a partner has that power over me," he admitted.

Morgan stared at him for a moment. "You're messing with my paradigms."

Leaning forward, he kissed Morgan again. "I have been in relationships with men well enough to know what my preferences are. Is that going to be a problem?"

"No, just...." Morgan closed his eyes and took a deep breath. Blinking them open, he continued. "I wasn't expecting for you to want to be a bottom."

"I might be a bit of a power bottom," he teased.

His lover smiled at him. "I can handle that." They kissed, harder this time, more demanding. They had agreed to have sex again. That turned him on more than he cared to admit.

Moving his hands along his partner's trim waist, Zach touched the top of his hips, waiting. Other than the initial heated kisses, he'd let Morgan control the sex. He didn't want to send him into a spiral, not after they'd already done so much.

The smaller man's groans and rocking hips told him he seemed at least open to this. Guiding his hands lower, he closed around the hard member. Still no panic. Stroking, he made slow movements. Morgan whimpered, low and soft.

"Is this okay?"

His partner nodded, and Zach sped up his ministrations in response.

"Can I touch you?"

"Yes." Zach punctuated the sentence with a high-pitched whine as Morgan grasped his new erection and rubbed his fingers along his frenulum.

Together, they stroked and teased and tested each other. What made the other one moan? Or grunt or squirm with pleasure. Zach came embarrassingly fast. Morgan took a bit longer, and Zach pushed the redhead onto his back, swallowing him deep as his lover lost his hot seed down his throat.

They lay together, struggling to catch their breath, when a knock sounded at the door.

"Fuck." Morgan covered his face with a pillow.

"I'll get it, then." Zach crawled out of bed, pulled on a robe, and located his wallet. The guy from room service attempted to bring the cart into the room, but he refused, mostly because of the clothes strewn about the room. Handing the server a ten as a tip, he let the man know they would put the cart outside when they were done.

The attendant smiled and disappeared down the hall without further comment. Wheeling the cart in, Zach set it in the middle of the room. He unfolded the desk into a makeshift table and set the food out.

"Dinner's here."

Morgan tentatively entered the room, he appearing a tiny bit dejected—he had also wrapped himself in one of the complimentary robes.

"What's wrong?"

"Nothing." Morgan smiled at him. "So, what's in the romance package?

"I think it's underneath." Checking the cart, he pulled out a bottle of champagne, a box of scented floating flower petals, and a half dozen chocolate-covered strawberries.

"Not bad," he commented setting the bottle on the table next to the food.

"Looks good." Morgan smiled at him, but it didn't reach the corners of his eyes like it had before.

"Let's eat?"

"Sure." Morgan took the desk chair, and Zach moved the big wing-back chair from the corner to the table. Zach devoured his food and drank two full glasses of champagne. His partner ate, too, but more slowly.

"Can I ask you a question?" Morgan pushed the last of his salad around on the plate.

"Of course." He took a sip of the excellent

champagne the manager had sent.

"Why don't you use your full name?" He focused on his food.

Reaching over, Zach hooked his fingers under his chin and pulled his face upward so he looked him directly in the eye. "Don't be afraid to talk to me and ask me things, Morgan. If we want this to work, even for tonight, then we need to be open and honest with each other. Okay?"

"Okay."

"And to answer your question, my religious parents named us all after important figures in the Bible or saints. My parents were early adopters of the quiverfull movement." Closing his eyes, he recited the Bible verse from long buried memories. "'Children are a heritage from the Lord, offspring a reward from him. Like arrows in the hands of a warrior are children born in one's youth. Blessed is the man whose quiver is full of them. They will not be put to shame when they contend with their opponents in court. Psalm 127.'" Opening his eyes, he saw Morgan, his brow furrowed. "It means that children are a blessing from God, and the more children you have the more blessings, and God will give you only as many as you can handle."

Morgan nodded, rubbing his fingers over his

forehead. "How many brothers and sisters do you have?"

"Full brothers and sisters, fifteen total, including me, but three sets of twins. I'm kid number seven. I've lost count of how many half or stepbrothers and sisters. My mother almost hemorrhaged to death after the second to last one, and the doctors told her she had to stop. She told them God would choose her path. She died giving birth to my youngest sister." He swallowed hard. "Fourteen at the time, I decided I didn't want to follow in my parents' footsteps. So, despite being homeschooled for most of my life, I made the decision to go to high school and get my diploma then moved away to go to university, and I haven't been back. I got made fun of a lot in high school for my name and my looks and my background, so I shortened my name to Zach and started playing sports to fit in and...." He shrugged. "I took a law course from this crusty old cop who was far too jaded, and I fell in love with the idea of being a police officer and helping people. After I finished my Bachelor of Social Work, I went and did police foundations in PEI and applied to anywhere hiring across the country. Since I grew up more or less bilingual, when Ottawa accepted my application, I jumped on it, and here I am."

"Wow."

Zach mentally beat himself up. "Sorry, that was a lot of verbal vomit you did not need."

Grasping his hand, his lover brought it to his lips and kissed his palm. "It's okay. I'm glad you told me. I take it you don't have a lot of contact with your family."

"Not much," he admitted. "I have two sisters who got out of the movement, and the youngest brother, but they're all back east. I invited my dad and his third wife to my wedding, and they responded by sending me a bunch of you're-a-sinner literature. That's the last time I tried."

"Um." Morgan stared at him. "You're married?"

Fuck. "Was," he replied. "We're divorced now. She then married my ex-boss."

"She?" His voice had gotten higher and face burned red.

Zach chewed on his lip. Butterflies pounded in his stomach. This, this reaction right here was a big part of why he chose not to be involved in the community. "Yes."

"You said you've had relationships with men." He sounded hurt.

"I've had both," Zach replied. "I consider myself

bi."

Morgan nodded but refrained from commenting.

"Is that a problem?"

"No, I...." His lover closed his eyes and took a deep breath before opening them "I was just surprised."

"Me, too. My co-worker's sister thought she was setting me up with a girl. That's why it took me a few minutes to come say hi. I debated bolting," he admitted.

"You? Afraid of me?" Morgan's eyes widened.

"Terrified, for a lot of reasons."

Leaning over the table, Morgan kissed him. "Don't be. This is one night. No pressure. And I don't believe in outing people."

"Thank you, it's complicated at work, and with my family." He shook his head.

"I'm sorry. I know how much it hurts."

Morgan squeezed his hand, and he squeezed back. "I take it your family isn't great either?"

"Kicked me out at seventeen. I haven't had much to do with them since," he replied. "Hence, the Misfits."

"I'm sorry."

"Me, too, and this is crazy heavy conversation for two people having a one-night stand." Morgan smiled at him. "So, how about those Sens?"

The question made him laugh and broke the uncomfortable tension. Leaning forward, Zach captured his temporary partner's lips. "Want to try out the rest of the romance package?"

"How do you suggest we do that?"

"How about we take a bath with those petals, since we never got around to having a shower?" He grinned. "Then we'll see what else we can get up to."

"Up?" his lover teased.

Zach's erection rubbed against the soft terrycloth fabric of the robe he wore. His desire to feel his temporary partner inside him drove him forward. "Or hard, which ever you prefer."

"You're insatiable," Morgan replied, but Zach pulled him to his feet and steered him toward the bathroom. His lover let out a low whistle at the at huge Jacuzzi tub in the middle of the room also furnished with a large shower, double sinks, and a separate toilet area. "Nice."

"Tell me about it, I wanted in the tub the second I saw it."

Kissing his partner, Zach dragged himself away and said, "I'm going to go to the bathroom. Can you handle drawing the bath?"

"Sure."

After using the facilities, he washed his hands as Morgan dumped the box of flower petals into the tub filling with steaming water.

"Are you sure those are safe to go in there?" he asked, sliding up behind Morgan, his growing erection pressed into the small of the other man's back. He watched his face in the mirror behind the tub.

"It says on the box." He held it for him to read. "Add entire box for a sensual experience. Safe for whirlpool and Jacuzzis."

"I hope the experience lives up to the promise."

"It has so far," Morgan whispered.

Zach kissed a spot on the side of his head. Reaching down, he loosened the tie on the terrycloth robe away and pushed the material off his shoulders, letting the robe pool on the floor.

He'd noticed the scars before but hadn't spent time on them. Now, standing behind Morgan, he examined the damage. The surgical scars stood out the most, next to irregular semicircular marks. Experience told him they'd been caused by steel-toed boots. He counted the marks—eight—that broke the skin anyway. Countless more had likely caused bone-crunching, tissue-crushing damage that didn't show through his scars. Marks on his jaw and along his arms. Defensive wounds on his hands. He catalogued them all. His heart broke a tiny bit more as he discovered each new scar.

At the base of his neck off to the left, a black semicolon stood out among the fading scars.

"I just noticed your tattoo." Zach traced the spot.

Morgan had gone oddly quiet as he stood in front of the bath, naked, emotional turmoil playing across his face as Zach watch him in the mirror.

His lover reached back and touched the small semicolon. He nodded. "Yeah. We match."

"When?"

Morgan swallowed underneath his touch. Hesitating.

"Sorry. Heavy conversation again. You don't have to—"

"No," he interrupted. "I want to tell you."

He pressed a kiss to the tattoo on the back of Morgan's neck. "Okay."

"After I was bashed. A couple of months after. No one warns you PTSD can show with a delay. I went through a bad time, and I had more than one...." He paused. "Suicidal ideation." He shrugged. "I got through it, and one of Phoebe's friends—this incredible trans guy, Nico—showed me his semicolon ink, and I liked the symbolism. The end of something, but not the end of everything." He glanced back at Zach. "You?"

"After my divorce. My wife cheated—bad enough—but she cheated with my boss. After it all came out, it turned out everyone had known, but no one told me, and once the depth of that particular humiliation set in, I went a bit off the rails. Didn't feel I had anyone in my corner."

Morgan turned in his arms and rose onto his tippy toes. They kissed, soft, hard, then soft again, Zach pushing his own robe away. "Can we get in?"

"Thought you'd never ask." Zach grabbed his hand, and, together, they stepped into the tub. He hissed as the hot water almost scalded his skin. It took a few moments before they both sank below the bubbles that the petals created. Reaching over, Morgan turned on the jets and adjusted them so they moved the water softly, without too much background noise.

Their legs tangled together, but their upper bodies remained separate. They relaxed in the hot water, leaning against the soft jets, the flower petals dissolving around them. He waited for his lover to give him a clear indication they could touch.

Morgan stared down at the bubbles and let out a heavy sigh.

"What's wrong?"

"It's okay if it's too much," he replied. "If you're turned off."

"What?" He grabbed Morgan and pulled him into his lap. They both faced the mirror on the wall. "Why the hell would you think that?"

"Once you saw the scars, I mean really saw them, you stopped touching me."

Zach flicked water at him. "You're clueless. I was waiting for you to say I could touch you. I don't know if you've noticed, but I'm trying very hard to take things at your pace here."

His shoulders sagged at his words. "Oh."

"If you want me to take charge, I will, though." He nipped at his ear. "Just tell me."

Morgan shivered. "I'll let you know." Sighing, he rested against him.

They stayed together, quiet, not talking. Morgan wiggled against him, and Zach's dick responded in kind.

"I almost want to fuck you right here," he mumbled.

"Water makes a horrible lube." Morgan turned

around slightly. "Plus, I think the condoms are in the bedroom."

"Fucking hate those things."

His partner stiffened. "Oh. Have you, um…?" He flushed red, and Zach suspected it had nothing to do with the temperature of the water.

"Had sex without condoms?" he offered.

"Yeah."

"Yes. My ex-wife and my ex-boyfriend from college. I was tested after each relationship ended, and again six months later, in the case of my ex-wife." Zach pressed a kiss to the side of his head. "Sorry. We should have had this conversation before falling into bed together."

"It's okay." Morgan cleared his throat. "I was with my ex-boyfriend for five years. We broke up, or were in the process of breaking up, when I got bashed. Straw that broke the camel's back so to speak." Zach pulled his lover's hand out of the water and kissed along his scarred wrist. "We tested before we were together, and we weren't always safe." Morgan took a deep breath. "I was tested during the medical follow-ups that happened. More than once."

"Standard procedure," he assured him. "Not everyone can or will admit if a sexual assault occurred."

Turning around fully so they faced each other, Morgan pressed their chests together, captured his lips, and they kissed. "You really don't remember my case?"

"No," he replied honestly.

"I remember you. It took me a bit to clue in. It was the first time I was being interviewed after being released from the hospital. There was a Sargent Berkowitz or Berko-something."

"Berkovich. I was taking over for him," he supplied.

"Yeah, and Sargent Lancaster, Rylie. He was nice. I mostly worked with him," Morgan explained. "I think you were observing. I met you for maybe a second before going into the interview room, and I remember thinking, who the heck is the Viking?"

"Would it amuse you to find out that Rylie is the one who set us up?"

"Really?" His eyes widened.

"Yeah, well, his sister. She met her boyfriend through Madame Eve. She thought I needed help getting over my ex."

"And?"

"And what?"

"Are you over her?" he asked coyly.

Grabbing his partner's hand, Zach guided him to his erection. "What do you think?"

"I think we need to get out of the water."

"Agreed." Morgan stood first and helped pull him to his feet. Grabbing towels off the rack, they dried off. He wrapped the material around his waist and sauntered into the bedroom before tossing the twisted sheet aside.

"What do you want?" he asked his lover as he joined him.

"You." Morgan shoved him backward onto the bed. Zach slid into position and allowed his lover to straddle his hips. He reached down and stroked their hard members together.

Letting out a gutted groan, Zach thrust his hips upward. "Please," he begged, not sure what he wanted.

"I want to enjoy this. It's not every day I get to fuck a Viking." His lover bit his lower lip then, moving back, he regarded him from the top his head to the tip of his toes, making Zach shiver with anticipation.

"What do you want to do to me, Morgan?"

Raising an eyebrow, he grinned. "I want to fuck you."

"What are you waiting for?" Zach growled. "I need your cock, now."

Giving their dicks one last squeeze, Morgan moved away from him and grabbed lube and a condom from his bag. Touch of lube, condom, more lube, lots more lube.

Climbing back into the bed, his lover crouched next to him. Zach firmly planted his feet on the bed, tilting his pelvis to offer a better angle.

Morgan applied lube to his entrance, rubbing in a circular motion, in a gentle, but insistent manner. Pre-cum leaked from his cock as he stroked himself, moans coming from the back of his throat as his partner slipped a single digit inside of him. He rubbed back and forth against the sphincter muscles, causing him to shake and twist under his touch. Morgan pushed in a bit more, hitting his prostate, and he called out, more pre-cum drooling down the side of his cock.

"Fuck me," Zach begged. "Please."

His lover smiled at him. "How?"

Zach's chest and face heated. "Can you take me from behind?"

Morgan paused, a lot of emotions played across his face, and he couldn't read all of them, but his partner nodded. "Yes, I can. Turn over."

It took a bit of reconfiguring, but Zach found himself hugging a pillow to his chest as he kneeled on the bed, Morgan behind him, fingering him.

Glancing back at the incredibly sexy redhead, he grinned. "I'm ready when you are."

Morgan swallowed. "Talk to me, okay? I can't see your face, so I need to know what you're feeling."

"I will," he promised. Taking a few deep steadying breaths, he waited. He let out an involuntary whimper as the head entered through the outer ring of muscle.

"Zach?" He stopped moving. "What's going on?"

"I'm okay." He focused on breathing in through his nose and out through his mouth. "It's been a little while for me. Go slow."

His partner pressed in a bit farther, and Zach's body protested. "Wait," he commanded, and Morgan stopped moving, instead rubbing his back.

"Push out as I go in, makes it easier," his lover reminded him.

"Okay." Zach nodded into the pillow, and Morgan slid his cock farther inside him, and he pushed back a tiny bit. "Stop." He said one last time. "How much is left?" Zach panted, rubbing his face against the cool pillow.

"About an inch." Morgan's voice seemed tense and tight. "Are you doing okay?"

He nodded. "I think you're bigger than I'm used

to."

"I'll take that as a compliment."

"I meant it as one." Zach squeezed his lover and sighed as he buried himself fully inside of him. He loved the feeling of being so full, so stretched. Morgan waited, longer than he wanted him to before his cock withdrew a couple of millimeters then re-entered him. His cock rubbed against his prostate, and he cried out. Together, they moved slowly, but built up a good rhythm. Every hard thrust made his body scream with pleasure. His legs grew weak, and he collapsed onto the bed, trapping his cock between his stomach and the sheets. Morgan grasped both his hands, pinning him to the bed as their bodies slammed together.

"Please," he begged, bucking backward. "Please. Harder...more."

"Fuck," his lover swore as he drove his hips into him. Holding him tight, he thrust hard and fast, pushing Zach over the edge as if a Mack Truck raced through his body.

Biting the pillow, he screamed, his cock spasming as he lost his load into the sheets.

Morgan clamped down his shoulder but didn't bother to muffle his orgasm as he grew stiff before collapsing onto his back. They both panted. His lover went to withdraw, but he stopped him.

"Wait," he said between gasps of. "I like feeling you inside me."

"Mmm," his partner moaned. "Did I hurt you?"

"No, you felt amazing," Zach said.

Morgan kissed his shoulder and slowly pulled out. He sighed with the release of pressure as his partner moved to one side.

Rolling over to face him, Morgan pulled him in close. They kissed. Breaking apart, he rested his forehead against his lover's. "That was perfect."

Morgan smiled at him. "It was pretty prefect."

He had to stop kissing to yawn. "God, you must think I'm old. It's"— he glanced at the night stand— "ten and I'm ready for bed."

"I'm exhausted, too." Morgan hesitated. "Physically and emotionally exhausted."

Zach brushed a tuft of his red hair away from his face. "Understandable."

"I need to go take care of this." Morgan glance down as his deflating erection, and the condom filled with cum. "I'll be right back."

He returned after a minute or two, with a warm facecloth, and it felt like heaven against Zach's skin. After a through wipe down, they reorganized the bed and tucked themselves in. He wanted to talk, find out more about him, his life and his wants, his desires, but, as Morgan's eyes grew heavy and his breathing even out, Zach realized none of it mattered, because he was falling in love.

Shit.

Chapter Six

Morgan

Morgan shifted onto his side, happy and half-awake. He'd never been a great sleeper, often making do with four hours a night, and had learned to lie still and rest, letting his mind wander. He wondered how long he'd been out since they'd pulled the blankets up over themselves, and squinted at the dim hotel alarm clock. Three in the morning.

He stretched, moving carefully so as not to wake Zach, then slid out from under the covers. He tiptoed out of the bedroom, found a glass in the bathroom and had a quick swallow of water, then made his way back to the bedroom.

"Not sneaking out on me, are you?"

Morgan smiled, sliding back under the covers. "Sorry. I didn't mean to wake you."

"It's okay. I enjoyed the show."

"It's dark."

"Not completely. C'mere."

A moment later, Zach wrapped his strong arms around Morgan and pulled him tight. Morgan closed his eyes and let the warmth and safety of the moment wash over him.

Then Zach shifted just so. The big man drew a lazy circle around Morgan's nipple with his thumb, and a hardness pressed against the small of his back.

When Zach nuzzled the back of his ear, Morgan chuckled.

"I take it you're not sleepy?"

"It's hard to be sleepy when you're, uh...."

"Hard?"

"Mmm." Zach slid his hands down Morgan's chest then nudged him over, sliding on top of him and covering him with his full weight.

And damn, but it felt good to have him there.

"What happened to being a power bottom?" Morgan said.

"I saw yours." Zach groped the bottom in question. "And now I want it."

"You already had it."

"There's having, and there's having."

"You can be kind of a dog, can't you?"

"Well, I do have a bone."

He laughed, but then Zach rubbed his hard-on, teasing between Morgan's cheeks, and the laugh turned into something more like a groan.

"So, do you have a preference?" Morgan asked, when he managed a breath again.

"Huh?" At least Zach had as much trouble concentrating.

"How do you want me, Mr. Viking?"

"Light on. On your back. I want to watch your face."

"So, in case I forget to tell you later, when you do that thing you just did with your voice? Super sexy."

"It's my cop voice."

"Feel free to serve and protect me as hard as you'd like."

Zach groaned at the pun, and Morgan took the opportunity to wiggle again, which ended conversation. He reached up, lit the bedside lamp, and threw the covers off the bed. Morgan rolled onto his back, staring at Zach and enjoying every moment of the view. He really did look like a freaking Viking, and Morgan felt very, very plunderable. He lifted one lean leg, swinging it around to press against Zach's side, nudging him.

Zach didn't need to be told twice. The big man grabbed the bottle of lube and walked on his knees between Morgan's legs. He put the bottle in his mouth and wagged his eyebrows when Morgan offered a small frown of confusion. A second later, when he'd thrown both legs over his shoulders, Morgan understood.

He took the lube and worked one finger into Morgan, gentling him with light pressure to test.

"I'm okay." Morgan bit down harder on his bottom lip. "More. Please." Had he ever been this hard in his life? He wanted Zach inside him, wanted to feel Zach's strength, to be with him. The anxiety and worry from before had fled the room, and, although it would come back, right now, he intended to allow himself to damn well enjoy his body. And Zach's. Who knew the sexiest thing in the world was being able to trust someone?

I never want him to go.

He tried to unthink the thought, but too late. It got out there. Luckily, Zach took the moment to add a second finger, and the sensation had him groaning again.

"Yes. That."

"Look at me," Zach said. Not quite in his cop voice, but close enough. Morgan obeyed, and the sheer hunger in the way the big man looked at him was so damn clear. They wanted each other. Not a pity-fuck. This was....

The opening of a condom wrapper drew him back again. Watching Zach's face as he rolled it onto his dick, he tried to burn the view into his memory. Sexy, dangerous, cop-Viking face.

Zach teased him with his fingers once more then lined his cock up.

The pressure of his head replaced his fingertips, and Morgan breathed out one, long moan while Zach leaned into him, sliding inch after thick inch into him at an angle that sent small tremors rocking along his body.

"Still with me?" Zach's neck flushed, and their gazes locked.

"Yes." Not just an answer, he gave permission, and Zach braced his arms to either side of his shoulders, leaning forward, rolling Morgan higher, and lowering himself farther into him.

"Oh God. Yes."

Zach's lips twisted into a slow smile. Confident bastard. Morgan squeezed. The smile faltered, and Zach grunted, his eyes fluttering.

"You...." Zach said, his voice gruff. "You teasing me?"

"Depends." Morgan squeezed again. "Is it working?"

Zach rolled his hips, and Morgan made a guttural, needful noise that would have embarrassed him had Zach not echoed him. They rocked together and increased from the softer, slower pace they'd begun. Morgan wrapped his legs behind Zach, pulling him down hard with every stroke, and Zach gripped his shoulders in return.

What had he said? There's having, and there's having.

And still their gazes locked.

I have never had this. He couldn't decide if he wanted to cheer or weep, but mostly he wanted Zach to keep going. Also, he'd lose it if he didn't get to come soon.

"Okay?" Zach checked in again.

Morgan realized he'd been looking without seeing. He managed a quick and a breathy, "Please."

"Yeah?" Zach said. "You ready?"

Morgan bit down, nodding. He slid his hand between their sweaty bodies, and the moment he touched his cock, he was right on the edge.

Zach drove into him, and it took more willpower than he knew he had to keep his eyes open and watch while his own release hit him. Zach smiled when he came, a smile accompanied by a long, low, exhalation as much a cry as a groan.

With Zach collapsed on top of him, and the heat of skin and sweat and cum between them, Morgan closed his eyes and caught his breath. In a second, he'd get them cleaned up. Right now, he wanted to hold onto this moment.

I've never had this.

****

The light behind the curtains grew brighter, but Morgan didn't move, enjoying the warmth of the man beside him. He'd slept again, with no dreams, something so rare he could barely believe it. Did it have anything to do with the big man who, even now, breathed the deep and even breaths of someone well and truly resting?

He turned his head on the pillow. When Zach slept, the more severe lines of his face softened. He was less intimidating, for sure, though maybe the bedhead had something to do with it. He wondered how hard Zach had to fight his cowlick.

He also slept with one arm up behind his head, which made for a very nice view. Arms like that were supposed to make you feel safe, not threatened.

And they did.

He took a deep breath, a shaky feeling in the middle of his chest he knew from long practice came only when he avoided thinking about things he didn't want to think about.

Zach's eyes opened. When he saw Morgan was awake, he gave a mock scowl.

"No fair," he said. "You don't get to watch when I don't know you're looking."

"I'm admiring the view," Morgan said. "And the cowlick."

Zach laughed, rubbing his eyes with the flat of his hand. He stretched, and his shoulders let out a loud crack. It didn't seem to bother him, though, so Morgan rolled with it.

He leaned in, put one hand on Zach's shoulder, and kissed him.

"Good morning," he said, pulling back just enough to be able to look him in the eyes.

"Good morning," Zach said. Mischief lit his eyes, and, a second later, he felt Zach exploring him beneath the covers. He crawled on top of the big man and determined that every part of Zach agreed it was a good morning. He was hard. Again.

Seriously, the man had stamina. He'd miss that, and—

Right. That thought again. He tried not to think it.

"As much as I hate to be the one to say this,"

Morgan said, after another deep kiss left him more than a little bit breathless, "checkout is at ten."

Zach offered a sly grin. "We have all morning."

"No, we had all morning. You slept all morning. As did I. It's nine forty-five. We have fifteen minutes to figure out where our clothes are and get dressed."

Zach jerked, looking to the small alarm clock by the side of the bed. "Well, fuck me."

"Been there," Morgan said. "Done that." But he winked when Zach raised an eyebrow of reproach.

"I don't want to get out of bed," Zach said. "I haven't slept like that in...." He shook his head. "I don't know the last time I slept so well."

"Me neither," Morgan said. Then, with a groan, he slid his body off the warmth of Zach and got out of the bed.

Zach whistled.

Morgan laughed. "Thank you." He glanced around. It looked sort of like a clothing store had exploded. How did one sock get on the bedside table, and where had his boxers...? He started hunting around. *Ah.*

He scooped his boxers from underneath the unused television cabinet. He supposed they had been a bit athletic with their undressing. He stepped into them then turned to see Zach watching him get dressed. The big guy hadn't moved at all.

"Tick tock," Morgan said.

"I feel a bit like Cinderella."

"Running away from the ball?"

"Wishing I belonged there, maybe."

"In my experience? The people who own the castles aren't very charming." He intended it to be a lighthearted comment, but, at Zach's little nod, he remembered what he'd said about his family. "We have more fun with the mice and the pumpkins. And the fairy godmothers."

"You mentioned yours," Zach said.

"Phoebe," Morgan nodded. "Not only my boss; one of my best friends. Though I'll still be in shit if I don't get to work on time."

"You're working today?"

"If you can call it working. I mean, yeah, of course we work. And we work hard. But we laugh most of the time. I start at eleven, shop opens at eleven-thirty. If I can find my...aha!" He scooped up an errant shoe.

"I can't imagine having that much fun at work."

"Well, you'd be welcome to laugh with the rest of us Misfits."

Zach's smile seemed a bit pained, and Morgan cursed himself. Totally the sort of thing he wasn't supposed to say at this point. There would be no glass slippers. The Viking doesn't run off with the retail clerk in a rainbow carriage all the way back to the Village.

He's not out. Stop it.

"You now have less than ten minutes," he said instead.

"Fuck." Zach finally got out of bed.

Getting dressed was a bit of an adventure—Zach's underwear had somehow gotten tossed behind the television cabinet, which Morgan couldn't quite remember happening—and, of course, watching Zach move around naked distracted in a delightful way. He had thighs as thick as tree trunks, and the way the muscles moved in his shoulders when he reached down for a sock made Morgan's mouth water.

They made it to the front desk barely on time.

Morgan put down the two keycards and smiled at the woman on duty.

"Sorry," he said. "We cut checkout a bit close."

She waved a hand. "No trouble." At least this woman seemed less uptight than the girl who'd checked them in.

"Just sign here," she said, sliding two sheets of paper to Morgan for the incidentals. He signed one for her without looking, pocketing his copy. She thanked them for staying.

That was it. Done.

They wandered to the large front doors of the chateau on inertia, then stopped.

Morgan turned to Zach. He had his hands stuffed in his pockets, his shoulders set so tight you'd think he waited to take down a suspect or something.

"Thank you," Morgan said.

Zach blinked. Whatever he'd been expecting, that hadn't been it.

"Uh," Zach said. "You're welcome?"

Morgan laughed, and the odd tension between them melted. Zach blushed—it suited him.

"The whole point of this for me was to make a strong memory. You gave me one. So, thank you."

Zach opened his mouth, seemed to reconsider, closed it, then opened it again and said, "I had a great time."

Morgan leaned forward, and when he saw Zach tense—*right, public place, lobby of a hotel*—he altered course and wrapped his arms around him in a tight hug. After a second, he returned the gesture, and Morgan took one last long inhale.

The man smelled amazing. Eau de Teutonic

Warrior.

Then, desperate not to ruin the moment, he pulled back, smiled, shouldered his bag, and walked out the door.

That way, the big guy wouldn't see him fighting off tears.

The cold air helped. By the time he'd gotten to the lights and crossed over to the Rideau Centre, Morgan had recovered some of his self-control. He decided he'd go get a coffee before he took the bus home. He had enough time for a hot drink and a shower before work. He stabbed the button and waited.

"A strong memory," he said, speaking to himself. At least in the Byward Market people spoke to themselves all the time. It was practically a requirement for someone walking alone. No one even blinked at him. "You wanted a strong memory? You got one."

The light changed.

Morgan crossed, echoes of the night before still replaying. Zach. Burly, handsome, a little bit dented, and closeted.

A smarter man than Morgan would have been more specific from step one. A strong memory, sure, but maybe he should have specified something in a "happy" rather than a "bittersweet."

He blinked again. The cold wind kept making his eyes run.

Yeah, that was it.

Chapter Seven

Zach

Zach watched Morgan turn away, walk straight out the doors of the chateau, and turn right, toward the Rideau Centre. He stood in the same place, waiting, for longer than he cared to admit. But he didn't come back. His temporary lover had made it clear, unless he stepped out of the closet, this would only happen one time. It hurt. A lot.

Finally, he acknowledged to himself Morgan wasn't coming back. Going out into the bitter cold, he nodded to the bellhop who flagged down a taxi.

"Where you go?" the man asked, with a thick accent.

"Elgin Street police station." He hoped he could talk Rylie into dropping him off at Lansdowne to pick up his car after work.

The cabbie started the meter. It wasn't far, and maybe on a regular day he'd just walk, but the bitter cold made him think twice.

The cabbie stayed silent for the quick trip down Elgin Street and—other than the driver running a red light, almost rear-ending three cars, and using his cell phone eight times—he counted it as a successful trip.

Zach tossed him a ten and a five and slid out, going in through the main public entrance. He grabbed his ID badge out of his bag and tapped it at the locked door to the right of the main entrance. The reader blinked green and allowed him into the bowels of the police station. He headed down to the locker room to shower and change into the backup suit he left there and to get his service weapon from the armory locker. He had left it over the weekend, knowing he would be away from home.

Storing his boots and jacket in his locker, he grabbed towels from the cabinet and wrapped one around his waist once he finished stripping off. Sliding his feet into his water shoes, he padded into the empty shower area. Picking a shower head in the corner, he scrubbed away the remains of cum and lube the facecloths missed, and the sweat, and Morgan's cologne.

Tears burned at the back of his eyes, and he let them fall, biting his lip. He wouldn't cry aloud in the echoing, empty room. He stood there longer than he wanted to admit before he finished getting clean.

Padding back to the locker, he dried off and put on

clean underwear from his spares there and shrugged into his dress shirt and suit before collecting his service weapon. His gun clipped onto his belt, he headed upstairs to his cubicle.

He waved to their unit secretary as he entered. She glanced at the time and raised an eyebrow but refrained from commenting. He escaped Rylie only because he chatted on the phone, to what sounded like his very needy witness.

When he sat down, the photo of him and BOTN caught his eye. Picking up the heavy frame, he spun around and tossed it into the trash can he shared with the desk on the other side of the cubicle. Turning back to his computer, Zach had exactly twenty-two minutes of peace before Rylie leaned against the edge of his cubicle. "So?"

"So, what?" Pressing send on the email he'd finished writing, he locked his computer and spun around to glare at the smug expression on his friend's face.

"How was she?"

"I don't kiss and tell."

"Bullshit."

"Ry," he warned.

"When are you going to see her again?"

He had to suppress the little bubble of anger, as he couldn't correct Morgan's gender. "I'm not."

"That bad a lay, eh?"

"No, I just—"

"Okay, so you slink in here at almost noon."

"It's barely eleven."

His best friend ignored the time correction. "Looking like you had one hell of a fucking night. Smelling like the locker room soap, wearing the emergency suit I know you hate, and you finally tossed out that stupid photo, and you're telling me you're not going to see her again?" He stared at him. "What the fuck did you do wrong?"

"Nothing," he snapped, raising his voice.

"It's got to be a whole heck of a lot more than nothing."

"Why does it always have to be on me? Why can't it be him that has the problem for once?" he yelled.

Rylie pulled back, blinking, his mouth gaping. "Uh."

"What?"

"Did you just say him?"

Zach felt all the blood drain from his face, and spots swam in front of his eyes. He slumped back against his chair before putting his head between his legs to try and prevent himself from passing out. His body went from cold to hot to cold all over again, and he suppressed the urge to vomit.

"Zach?" Rylie knelt in front of him. "Are you okay?"

He nodded and shook his head then nodded again. "I don't know," he whispered.

"Is there something you're trying to tell me?"

"I...."

"Zach." His best friend grasped his hands. "Look at me, okay?" Forcing himself to lift his head, he looked his friend in the eye. "I don't care okay. You're my best friend," he murmured.

"But—"

"But nothing. I wouldn't be doing this job if I judged people on their skin tone or religion or their sexuality." Rylie paused. "Are you gay?"

"No."

"Zach—" Ry started, but Zach held up his hand.

"I'm bi. I have dated both women and men in the past." The words came easier than he'd thought they would. "But, yes, last night I went on a date with a guy, and it was amazing."

"So, why the hell aren't you seeing him again?"

"I...." The excuse that he was in the closet, afraid

to come out at work, afraid of being judged by his co-workers and his friends, evaporated in front of him. He had been rejected by his family long ago, and it didn't matter as much as it once had. "I don't know."

"You're an idiot. I hope you know that." Rylie stood and shook his head. "You need to go find your balls."

"You're right."

"Excuse me?" Ry stared at him.

"You're right," Zach stood. grabbed his suit jacket off of the back of the chair, and shrugged into it.

"Where are you going?

"To find my balls," he called over his shoulder. "And maybe a boyfriend." He ran down the three flights of stairs and out into the bitter cold. Zach didn't have a home address, nor a phone number for Morgan. What he did know was his shift started at eleven at Urbane Myth—his only chance with him. The ten-block run took him less than eight minutes. He dodged across traffic and ignored how the snow and slush soaked his dress shoes. Skidding to a stop outside the unassuming shop, he took in two big gulps of bitter-cold air before entering.

The door jangled, and the front appeared deserted. They weren't open yet, he supposed. He could make out Morgan's voice from the back of the store and headed that way. He stopped just outside the door, which was ajar, and peeked inside.

Morgan sat in a big cushy chair, and a woman stood over him. She could only be Phoebe, and fit Morgan's description of "glamazon" to a T.

"Repeat after me," she intoned.

Morgan groaned. Finally, he nodded.

"I am not stupid," she said.

"I am not stupid," he repeated.

"I am worth the love and attention of a good man," she said.

"Phoebe."

She put her hands on her hips. "Say it."

"I am worth the love and attention of a good man." Morgan smiled, and Zach's stomach did a huge somersault. Any doubts disappeared from his mind.

"And what are closets for?" Phoebe asked.

Stepping into the back of the store, Zach answered for his lover. "Clothes. They're for clothes."

Morgan

"Earth to Morgan."

Morgan flinched. He knew he looked guilty, and he'd never get it past Phoebe.

"Sorry."

She tapped his forehead with one manicured fingernail. "Where are you today? You've been spacing out ever since you got here."

They worked at the back of the L-shaped store, near the fitting stands. Phoebe slipped one of her awesome shawls on a mannequin, tying an expert knot. Morgan had been halfheartedly sorting some of the paperwork at the small desk. Phoebe hated paperwork, and he had a knack for it. For some reason, he enjoyed the challenge of balancing the orders for fabrics, threads, and other supplies with vendor minimums and the various sources. He realized, though, he'd been staring at a single invoice for a full five minutes without doing anything.

"Sorry," he said. "My mind is wandering. What did you want?"

"I want you to go through the consignment orders and give everyone a call. I got a lot done this weekend, and the sooner they get the call, the sooner they come in and pick up their frocks, and the sooner I get paid." She raised an eyebrow. "And we all know how I feel about getting paid."

No one resisted Phoebe in a good mood, and today she was in a great mood. Urbane Myth didn't often get busy after Christmas, but she had garnered some online attention after a great vintage costuming show she'd taken part in, which trickled down to some store traffic. Spring would mean weddings, too, and she was getting a jump on some custom gowns and suits.

In short? The store looked great. On the women's side, killer Phoebe-original dresses lined the display. Each designed and handmade by Phoebe: fashion and function for body types you'd never see on a runway. The smaller, men's side had less range, but, again, Phoebe had come up with gorgeous outfits. Every design could be customized, and the pins holding the garments together on the dummies somehow gave the illusion of completeness, even though Morgan knew everything would need a fitting before someone took home one of Phoebe's creations.

He loved the store. He loved the clientele, too, many of them queer folk like himself. Phoebe had filled a niche she'd found empty herself: clothing for bodies outside the typical. Her trans community loved what she designed, and it hadn't been long before the bears had shown up when they needed something formal—bears in kilts, it was a thing—and from there, her line had taken off. If she had the time, Phoebe was up for the challenge. She'd even gotten some small positive newspaper space with her suits tailored for women who didn't want to go to any wedding in a dress—not even their own.

Working at Urbane Myth reminded him of everything he had, as opposed to the things he had lost.

"You're doing it again."

"Sorry!" Morgan shook his head. "I'm sorry. Consignment orders. On it."

"No, you're not." She took his shoulder. "What is it?"

"It's kind of silly."

"I love silly."

"I'm maybe crushing out on someone who is very wrong for me."

Phoebe pulled one of two chairs from in front of the fitting area and sat down. She crossed her hands in her lap and raised one eyebrow again. "Dish."

Morgan swiveled in the plush desk chair. "So, you know how I went on that date?"

"Yes. Your big 'Make a new memory' plan, where you checked in late." She leaned back. "Wait. Did you...make a new memory?"

"You make it sound filthy." Morgan tilted his head.

"But, yeah. A big, filthy memory. Multiple memories, heavy on the filth. Like, thanks for the memories, but I'm a bit sore now."

Phoebe fanned herself with one hand. "I love this story."

"Yes, well." Morgan grimaced. "There's a slight problem."

"He's not your type?"

"God no. He's funny. He's nice. Employed. And it doesn't hurt that he's, like, six-foot-forever, a wall of muscle. He's…. You know those romance novel covers with the guys who look like Vikings with access to good dentists and a hairdresser?"

Phoebe nodded.

Morgan tapped his nose.

"I'm not seeing the downside here, kiddo."

"Well, the agency I used matches people for a night—" How to explain the rest? She wouldn't be thrilled.

"So, he's against relationships? Or…is he a sex worker? Is it a consort agency? Because, honey, you know you can have a relationship with a sex worker, right? Work is separate from play."

"No, he's not a prostitute. Quite the opposite. He's a cop."

"Oh." Her smile faded, which shouldn't have surprised him. Cops and queers rarely made best friends. "Still," she said, "surely even cops are allowed to date?"

"He's not out," Morgan said. "Not to mention his family is super religious, which I guess explains the not-out part. And there's his job—though he is with the Hate and Bias Crimes Unit and his ex-wife who cheated with his ex-boss, but that's a whole other story, and maybe it's dumb for me to wonder if—"

Phoebe held up a hand. "Say no more."

Morgan exhaled. "I feel stupid."

She rose, took him by the shoulders, and turned him to face her. "You are not stupid."

The bell over the front door jingled.

"I should go." Morgan turned toward the front of the store.

"Let them wait a second." Phoebe squeezed his shoulders, her brown eyes full of equal parts compassion and determination. "Repeat after me."

Morgan groaned, but Phoebe didn't relent. So he nodded, knowing she'd never let him up from the chair if he didn't.

"I am not stupid," she said.

"I am not stupid." He tried to make it sound

convincing.

"I am worth the love and attention of a good man."

"Phoebe."

"Say it."

"I am worth the love and attention of a good man." This came out stronger, and Morgan felt his lips quirk upward.

"And what are closets for?" Phoebe said.

Morgan opened his mouth, but another voice replied.

From behind them, Zach Boyd said, "Clothes. They're for clothes."

They both turned. Phoebe gave Zach a slow, appraising look that Zach returned in equal measure. Morgan stood, then resisted the urge to step back. Unsettled, he half expected one of them to leap at the other, and that would end poorly.

And he totally didn't think Zach would come out on top.

"You're Phoebe," Zach said.

"And you're the Viking?" Phoebe replied.

"Yep."

Zach cleared his throat. "Can I talk to you?"

"I think I'll go to the front desk. Call the consignment orders." Phoebe narrowed her eyes at

Morgan. "Remember. Worth it." She left before Morgan could say another word.

Zach looked good, if professional. A white button-down, striped navy tie, and navy suit jacket and pants. Wet snow clung to his dress shoes. His face and hands were reddened with the cold, and he wore a gun on his hip. His chest heaved.

"It's minus twenty outside. Where's your coat?"

"I didn't stop to put it on." Zach shrugged. "I ran from work—"

"You *ran*?"

"Yes. It's only ten blocks." He bit his lip. "The thing is, I want to see you again."

"Oh." He gathered his thoughts. "Look, Zach. I had a great time. I did. And I like you. I think you're incredible. And in different circumstances—"

"Such as?" Zach said.

He was not making this easy.

"You know what I mean," Morgan said.

"The coming out thing?"

"Yes," Morgan said. "The coming out thing. Look, I understand why you're not out, and I would never pressure you to do so, but that isn't the kind of life I want to have, and—"

"I came out."

Morgan blinked. "What?"

"At work. With my partner. Well, with my partner, the receptionist, and maybe a few other people who overheard me. There is little doubt the news about my being bi is spreading as we speak. I was kind of loud."

"Loud?"

Zach shook his head. "Doesn't matter. Thing is, they know. And the world didn't end. I know there's more to coming out than telling some co-workers, but...." He shrugged. "It's like the semicolon. It's done, and forward is the only way. It's where I'm going."

What the big blond man just said started to sink in. "You came out."

"Started to," Zach said. "And it's not for you. Or, okay, not just for you. It's for me. I want this. I want you." He grinned. "I've always known I'm bisexual. I always put myself leaning more toward women, but that doesn't mean I'm not willing. You know, to explore a relationship with you."

"Zach—"

"I want to go skating, and I want more bubble baths, and I want to climb with you, and I want to be a Misfit."

"Zach—"

"Please, Morgan, hear me out."

"Zach—"

"I don't want you to think I'm rushing into this, or that I haven't thought it through."

"Oh my God, stop!" Morgan said.

Zach blinked.

"Dude, I'm trying to get you to shut up so I can kiss you."

"Oh." Zach blushed. "Okay."

Morgan rolled up on his toes and kissed him. Zach's chin was a little rough with stubble and his cheeks still cold, but as he slipped his tongue between Zach's lips and wrapped his arms around the big man's neck, he didn't care a bit about a little beard rash.

From the front of the store, Phoebe offered polite applause. No doubt she'd heard every word.

"Okay," she said. "He'll do."

Epilogue

"So, I want to thank you all for coming to our first official turn at hosting Christmas for the Misfit Toys," Morgan said, raising a glass. He still didn't drink often, but the bubbly was a rare treat.

Their guests raised glasses around their packed apartment. Phoebe had brought Dennis, the woofy hipster otter boy she'd been seeing. Johnny and Matt sat on the couch, already mid-snuggle. Fiona had done her annual rant about the vile lyrics of "Baby It's Cold Outside," and Jenn had suggested they put on *Scrooged*, which played in the background, unwatched. No Haruto or Nick this year—Haruto's dad was sick, and Nick seemed to be off everyone's radar thanks to his new boyfriend Erik.

But the best part was seeing the new faces. Even though they'd had places of their own to go, Zach's co-worker Rylie had shown up with his sister, Amy, who'd brought her fiancé, Jasper. Watching the four interact with the sometimes overpowering group of Christmas Misfits had been...interesting. He didn't think Jasper had met a trans woman before, and Phoebe continued to be a force of nature unto herself. Turned out, Amy could more than hold her own, though, and she and Phoebe had joined up in a joint effort to make Jasper squirm as often as they could.

They fit right in.

Morgan met Zach's gaze and read the little signs of his nervousness. You'd have to know him to see the strain in his smile, or the way he held his glass, or the ramrod shoulders. Morgan wondered just how worried Zach had been about hosting this party.

Zach winked at him.

Aw.

The party had been Morgan's idea, and maybe Zach had seemed overwhelmed at the thought of hosting the annual event, but he'd come around to it. Zach knew it mattered to him, and, though he said he'd had big plans for their first Christmas together, they had the whole day ahead of them tomorrow.

It had been close, but three solid days of Morgan and Zach racing to put everything to rights once they'd found the place meant no moving boxes in sight. They'd moved in almost a month earlier, but, between Christmas retail at Urbane Myth and Zach's work schedule, things had piled up.

Morgan hoped no one wanted a tour of the

bedroom. More than a few boxes had ended up tossed in there when they'd run out of steam last night and thrown themselves into bed long past midnight.

"Before we break out into the traditional ornament game, I did want to say a few words."

Fiona booed.

"I promise, there are only a few," Morgan said.

She grinned.

"We generally get together and goof off and have fun, and that's important. But this last year, I've realized it's just as important we remind each other of the big stuff, too. Family is supposed to be this amazing bond nothing can break, and as we all know it's not always the case. But you guys? You're my family. The real one. The one that counts, sticks by me, and gives me shit when I screw up but still loves me anyway. You guys were there when I was broken, and you guys stuck by me until I got myself more-or-less back together. I don't know if I ever said thank you, so I'm saying it now. I wouldn't be here without you."

Morgan looked at Zach, and he saw the big man's eyes fill. Things hadn't gone great with a lot of his family, either. Some of his sisters, the ones who'd gotten away from his family, had been pretty cool when he'd come out to them, though. He'd wanted to remind Zach of the people he had right here in the room.

It mattered.

"Okay," Morgan said. "Enough sentimental crap. I know why you're really here. Time for the ornaments."

They all brought ornaments, and everyone left with one after a game involving unwrapping, swapping, or stealing the various baubles. Often, some of the ornaments ended up being somewhat pornographic. Morgan hoped for another dildo-wearing snowman for his collection.

"Before that," Zach said, surprising him by speaking up—and eliciting more over-the-top boos from Fiona. "It's not everything." He pulled a small box out from his pocket. Black velvet. Small. Hinged.

Oh. My. God. Morgan stared. His mouth opened.

"See, I planned for a quiet Christmas Eve," Zach said. "But you decided to host a big party. I had to change my plans. I guess it makes the family here witnesses." Zach stepped up to him and then went down on one knee.

Morgan snapped his mouth closed.

"So." Zach opened the box, revealing a simple gold band. Understated. Simple.

Perfect.

Zach looked up at him, took a deep breath, and—

"Yes!" Morgan blurted.

Zach smiled. "You didn't let me ask."

"Hurry up, then."

"Morgan, will you—"

"Yes!"

"Marry me."

Morgan reached down and dragged Zach back to his feet then rocked onto his toes for a kiss, arms around Morgan's neck. They didn't come up for air for quite a while.

Everyone laughed and applauded, but Morgan could barely hear it. He met Zach's eyes, smiling so much his cheeks hurt.

"I also got you brand new skates," Zach said. "They're under the tree. We can go skating on the canal."

"You're sort of amazing."

"What do you think?" Zach said. "Our first Christmas. This a big enough memory?"

Morgan lifted himself onto his toes again, putting his lips right to Zach's ear.

"When it comes to you? Everything is big enough."

For more information about Project; please visit

https://projectsemicolon.com.

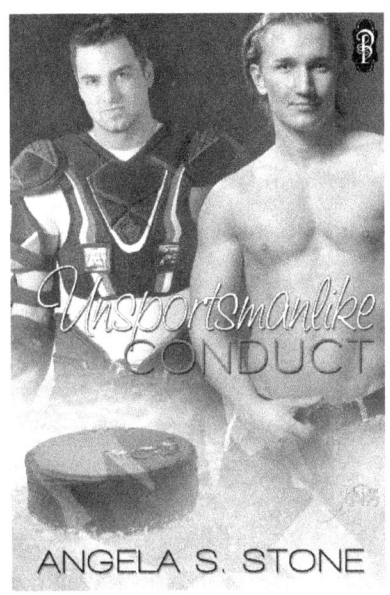

Chapter One

Owen looked up from his position next to the boards. The boys on the ice were doing a drill, and TJ showed off in top form as she sent pucks flying left and right. The next two rapid-fire shots deflected off her mask. Scott Alder, team captain and TJ's boyfriend, snapped the last puck right at her head. Everyone stopped when she pulled her mask off, her hand going to her forehead. The trickle progressed from a slow ooze to streaming through her fingers in a few seconds. *Shit.* He skated toward his goalie. Scott screamed for Jon, the trainer, and followed him.

They took TJ's arms and hurried her off the ice, her face and the front of her practice jersey already crimson. They had almost made it to the locker room when Jon arrived from the bowels of the arena.

He took one glance at TJ and ordered someone to get the team doctor. "Bring her into the medical room." They helped her through the changing area and into the medical office. Scott picked her up and set her on the trainer's bench, ignoring her grimace.

Jon grabbed a towel and wiped the blood away then applied pressure to the wound. "What happened?"

"She took a couple of pucks off the mask. Something must have cut her," Scott explained.

"The edge of the fiberglass did," TJ said, her voice muffled by the material. "They're still doing final adjustments on my new mask. I didn't get a chance to re-position before the second puck hit."

"I'm so sorry," Scott reached over and squeezed her arm. "I should have waited to shoot." Owen smiled at the couple. Finding someone who shared and understood the life and drive of a hockey player was special. He pushed down a tiny ping of jealousy and focused on his friends.

"It's just a small cut." TJ squeezed Scott's hand. "Not your fault. I should remember to use my catcher more often."

Scott laughed, short and bitter, but didn't let her go. Jon wiped up more of the blood. The profuse bleeding had stopped, but the wound still dripped. He reapplied a clean towel above her eye. "Why don't you guys go back out on the ice? The doc will come stitch her up, and she'll be fine."

Scott shook his head but narrowed his eyes at Owen. "I'll see you guys there."

Owen patted TJ on the pads before he left. The group of players swarmed around him when he stepped onto the bench.

"How is she?" Todd Korbel asked, his forehead furrowed with worry.

"She's all right, nasty cut above her eye. Facial wounds bleed like a son-of-a-bitch," he replied. "Let's go finish practice. She'll be stitched up and as good as new by the time we're done."

A few guys grumbled, but they all went back to

their drills. When one of their assistant captains gave them an order, they followed it.

The players wrapped up the formal part of the practice and while they scrimmaged with Ian as their goalie, Owen headed into the locker room to check on his teammates. Some of TJ's pads were in her locker but not all of them. Concerned she remained in the medical room, he walked in without knocking.

TJ lay on top of Scott, kissing him. He paused for moment, not wanting to interrupt, but the bang of the guys coming off the ice told him he had to. He shut the door behind him with a loud slam and cleared his throat. They pulled apart, and TJ grabbed Scott's hockey jersey, trying to cover up what Owen had already seen. "If you two are going to fuck, you should at least lock the door."

"Fuck off, Cartsy." Scott threw a loose glove at him.

"I'm just saying, you're lucky I'm not Coach. You'd give him an aneurism to go along with the heart attack he had when he found out about you two." He laughed as TJ flipped him the bird. "We're done with practice, so finish up and hit the showers before the guys wonder what got you all sweaty."

He slipped out and locked the door behind him. A

dull thud, another piece of equipment hitting the door, made him laugh again. Scott and TJ were lovesick, but they had it really bad for each other if they were doing it in the medical room.

Owen strolled to his locker, chuckling, and stripped off. He wasn't scheduled for conditioning, so he could hit the showers and go back to his apartment for a nice, relaxing night. He needed some rest before their next road game on Friday.

A couple of guys trickled in from the ice, and the two lovebirds emerged from the trainer's room a bit more presentable. He averted his eyes as TJ stripped down. It had been a bit awkward when she first arrived after being traded. She was more comfortable naked around them than they were around her. Once they'd had a big meeting and she flat out told them to deal with it, everyone mellowed out about the idea of having a girl in the locker room.

He didn't care. Most of the guys fell all over TJ, but she didn't do anything for him. Wrapping a towel around his waist, he grabbed his stuff and padded into the shower room. She followed.

He focused on washing up, while she picked a shower head, leaving several between them. Owen fixed his gaze on the tile wall, but stared at her when she hissed. "Okay, TJ?"

"Yeah, stupid stitches burn." She turned so water bounced down her chest and ran off her perky breasts, rather than over her face. If Owen were into that sort of thing, he would be harder than fuck at the moment

"Keep them away from the water. They shouldn't get wet," He'd been injured enough times to know the drill.

"Yes, Dad." She tilted her head forward and winced as water hit her stitches.

He finished up then dried off a bit and wrapped a towel around his waist. TJ kept leaning forward and back, only to pull away and whimper as lather poured into the new wound. "You need some help?"

She narrowed her eyes at him, but then nodded. "Can you rinse while I tip my head back?"

"Sure." Owen sauntered over to her, standing to the side. She held still as he rubbed the last of the blood away. "Scott is going to be jealous."

TJ laughed. "Like he could control himself. Ever notice how he won't shower with me?" She shut off the taps, tucked a towel around herself, and wrapped another around her hair. "Thanks for the help."

"No problem."

The second they were out, Scott headed into the

showers.

TJ giggled, winked at Owen, and wandered off to her locker, exchanging joking comments with the rest of the guys. Although most were half-dressed, they treated her like any other team member and she responded in kind. He pulled on his boxers and his T-shirt and sat at his locker.

Todd came out of the shower. "So, Owen, who's the girl you're seeing tonight?" Half the room snickered. He rolled his eyes. Sure he went on frequent dates. That didn't mean he slept with all of them—or any of them, for that matter. "Leaving on a road trip tomorrow, in case you forgot."

"I remember. I've got to make sure I leave Natalie a happy woman." Todd dodged the balled-up towel TJ threw at him from across the room.

"Watch it. That's my best friend you're talking about," she called. "You satisfy her lately?"

"Yes, ma'am. Three times last night."

The whole room groaned.

Ian leaned forward, still dressed in his goalie gear. "So Owen, when are you going to find that special girl?"

Oh great, not this again. "I had one on Monday night, thanks." He grabbed his jeans, dressing as quickly as possible in order to escape the rest of the conversation.

Ian reached into his locker, pulled out piece of paper, and tossed it to him. "How about finding one who might stick around for more than ten minutes after you finish?"

Montréal Castillo Hotel and Spa. Dammit! Of course they would try and set him up with someone through the 1Night Stand dating service. He'd played a key role in hooking up Scott and TJ, as well as Todd, Ian, and Natalie, but that didn't mean he wanted them to fix him up with some girl.

"No, no way. I told you from the outset Madame Eve was not going to hook me up with anyone."

Scott came out of the shower room, and he waved the card at him. "Please tell me you had nothing to do with this."

Scott held his hands up in innocence. "Talk to Tarah and Natalie. I don't even know how to get in touch with her."

TJ shrugged. "It was all Todd and Ian."

Todd gave him a shit-eating grin.

Ian, his partner in crime, smirked. "Her name is Addison, seven o'clock in room 1018. Make sure you bring rubbers."

He groaned, great, they trapped him into a date already. "Fine, but don't be surprised if nothing happens."

"Come on. Madame Eve will work her magic and, poof, you'll have yourself a perfect girl." Todd patted him on the shoulder.

Owen nodded. "Yeah, sure." He stuffed the card into his jeans pocket, shoved his feet into his shoes, and grabbed his jacket as he tore out the door, not looking back. In the solitude of the car, he let his shoulders slump. How could he tell his best friends a perfect girl didn't exist for him? He closed his eyes and rested his head on the steering wheel. He wanted the perfect guy.